A
Harlequin
Romance

THE
DOCTOR'S CIRCLE

by

ELEANOR FARNES

HARLEQUIN   BOOKS

Toronto • Canada   New York • New York

THE DOCTOR'S CIRCLE

First published in 1970 by Mills & Boon Limited,
17 - 19 Foley Street, London, England

Harlequin Canadian edition published June, 1971
Harlequin U.S. edition published September, 1971

Standard Book Number: 373-51497-2.

CHAPTER ONE

SHE stood on the pavement surrounded by her suitcases, parcels and bags, deciding what to do.

It was annoying that there had been nobody to meet her train. It was the fault of the airline, for her plane had been delayed for an hour and a half in Switzerland. Annoying, too, that by the time she had all her luggage out of the train, the station taxis had been taken and had disappeared. She rang up the Tudor Rose, but there was no answer; by the time she and her luggage were out on the pavement, even the private cars which might have given her a lift had gone.

Gabrielle Knight had been out of the country for three years, with only an occasional flying visit back to see her family. Now she was home for good, enthusiastically prepared to work in the family hotel.

It was the golden hair catching the light of the spring sunshine which also caught the attention of the man in the car. He drew in to the kerb, leaned across to open the near-side window, and said:

'Are you being met, or do you want a lift?'

'I was hoping one of the station taxis might come back.'

'They only come to meet the trains. There isn't another for nearly two hours. Which way are you going?'

'To the Tudor Rose on Mereworthy Lake.'

'I go right past it. Shall I take you?'

'Yes, please.'

He got out of the car and loaded all her baggage. He drove off, avoiding the High Street, obviously familiar with the town, and putting his foot down on the accelerator when he was out on the country road.

'This is kind of you,' said Gabrielle Knight.

'Pleasure,' Dr. Huwlett replied briefly.

Not one of the chatty ones, Gabrielle decided, and she relapsed into silence; but after a while, feeling she owed him at least a little conversation as token of her gratitude, she said:

'Lovely to be back in England again. The air is so beautifully soft . . .'

'Where have you come from?' he asked.

'Switzerland. I was working there for a year. Before that, Italy and France.'

'What kind of work?'

'Hotel work. I'm a receptionist. Lately, I've been at one of the big Zurich hotels.'

'You'll find the Tudor Rose rather small fry after that.'

'Oh, shall I?' There was a hint of amusement in her voice. 'Do you know the Tudor Rose?'

'I've known it all my life,' he said drily. 'From the outside.' There was a pause, and she hoped he was going to tell her why he did not know it from the inside, but all he added was: 'I'm told it's a very good and comfortable hotel. You should enjoy working there.'

'Good,' said Gabrielle, managing to suppress that hint of amusement, but wondering why, if he had known the Tudor Rose all his life, he did not also know her. He certainly looked vaguely familiar to her, but she made no pretence of knowing all the people in the neighbourhood. She had been away so much: boarding school, finishing school, and then work.

Her driver had fallen silent again and this time she left him in peace. The car swept along the country road, the man obviously knowing each bend and corner intimately, and came to the lake, a long expanse of water surrounded by low hills, lying placid and slightly misty on this day of misty

6

yellow sunshine. In a few minutes they came to the Tudor Rose.

It was a grey stone building, but everything had been done to make it an attractive place. Windows, doors and barge boards were painted white; climbing plants covered a good deal of the stonework, forsythia blazed along the front, and ranks of daffodils were massed round the forecourt, where there was room for a great many cars.

'This is it,' said Dr. Huwlett, sweeping up to the front entrance. 'They've certainly made the most of it; and see what a beautiful outlook it has.'

'Yes,' said Gabrielle. She got out of the car, and stood looking. Only the roadway between the lake and the hotel, and the lake so calm that it reflected the hills on the other side. A lovely silence. A slight breeze causing the daffodils to nod. The branches of the trees around the hotel tinged with spring green. 'Yes,' she said again, 'it's beautiful.'

He had unloaded her bags and put them on the wide step.

'Well, good luck,' he said to her.

'Thank you. And thank you very much for bringing me. Perhaps I shall see you again.'

'In one way, I hope not,' he said, and smiled at her; and that smile was so friendly and warm, so fraternal and kindly, that it cancelled the apparent unfriendliness of his words. He raised a hand to her in good-bye, got back into his car and drove away.

He drove on, beyond the Tudor Rose, followed the curve of the road away from the lake as it skirted the estate of the Misses Medlicott, came back to the water later and arrived at his own house at the other end of the long lake from the Tudor Rose. Farther on from the doctor's house, along a narrow valley between hills, bungalows and small houses began to appear; then came the old village of dark stone, bare and unattractive, whose people had always been poor. Further on still was the industrial town which owed its life to the mines, and was dying as the pits died.

This was a far cry from the peaceful lake and the unspoiled hills and the beautifully-maintained Tudor Rose. Gabrielle left her baggage on the wide step and went into the large lounge hall. It lay serene in the sunshine, with its red carpet, shining brass and copper, staircase curving up from the back of the hall, and flowers everywhere.

'Anybody home?' she called. 'Anybody home?'

A door at the back of the hall opened, and two women came hurrying towards Gabrielle. Her mother and her father's sister, hugging her, kissing her cheek.

'Welcome home,' said her mother. 'Lovely to see you. Whatever happened to you? We met the last two trains.'

'I was held up for an hour and a half at Zurich. I rang you from the station, but no reply.'

'We stayed shopping in the town. Mary was here, but I expect she'd left the desk for something.' Mary was a member of the staff.

'Come and have tea, Gay. We're in *our* little room. Jim will take all your stuff up to your room.'

'I'll freshen up first and then join you,' said Gabrielle, and went upstairs looking about her with pleasure, noticing how well-kept the whole place was, delighting in her own room which held her personal possessions and a mass of spring flowers. It was a corner room which usually held hotel guests but which, from now on, would be exclusively Gabrielle's. It had a window overlooking the lake and a side window with a view across the garden to the small woodland. The trees here were deciduous, turning glorious colours in autumn but now showing green in only a few places. On the broad hills across the lake, the Forestry Commission had cut wide swathes here and there on the hillsides

8

and planted pine and spruce and fir, their dark green showing clear cut on the dun colour of the hills. Soon the hills too would be green, but with the softer, lighter green of the new season's grass. 'It's a beautiful, beautiful place,' thought Gabrielle, as she thought every time she came back to it.

When she went downstairs again, her father had joined his wife and sister for tea. He stood up to kiss her, told her how well she looked and how good it was to have her back.

'Nice to *be* back, Dad. Are you busy at the moment?'

'Not very. Easter was a mad rush, as you can imagine. Whitsun is going to be too, by the bookings. But it's always a bit quiet between the two. Give you time to get your hand in.'

'The restaurant keeps us busy,' said her mother. 'We get a lot of outside people for lunch and dinner.'

'We've got something of a reputation for our food,' said Gabrielle's Aunt Catherine.

They talked to her about the hotel and the business it was doing, and Gabrielle sat back listening and sipping her tea, and realized that it was because they were all doing a job they were enthusiastic about that they were all so alive and so interesting. Her father, William Knight, was now sixty-two, but fit and tough and hard-working. Gabrielle was the daughter of his second wife, Pamela. Pamela, ten years younger than he, might easily have been thought twenty years younger, slim and pretty and lively as she was, her hair so skilfully dyed a soft brown for years, her figure so arduously kept slim.

It was Aunt Catherine, her father's sister and four years older than he was, who never bothered much about her appearance or age beyond being neatly turned out, and who looked all of her sixty-six years.

'By the way,' said her mother, 'how did you get here? Taxi?'

'No. By the time I'd coped with luggage, because the man-of-all-work collecting tickets was busy, and then phoned you from the booking office, everything had disappeared, taxis, cars, the lot. But a man in a grey Rover took pity on me and stopped to give me a lift. Brought me right to the door.'

'Nobody we know?'

'Nobody *I* know. You might. Or might not, because he said he'd known the Tudor Rose all his life, but only from the outside.'

'Must be a local, then,' said Mrs. Knight.

'Must be a teetotaller,' commented Aunt Catherine.

Gabrielle laughed.

'Mr. Holmes has a grey Rover,' said her father. 'Farms up in the hills. Burly man, speaks with a kind of country burr.'

'Not this one, Dad. Very cultivated voice.'

They held a mental survey of the grey Rovers they knew, but as none of them seemed to belong to the kind stranger with the cultivated voice, they gave it up and forgot about him. Even Gabrielle, who soon became absorbed in her work and met so many people in the course of it that one quiet man in a car was easily forgotten.

Ivor Huwlett, having reached his house at the end of the lake, turned his car on to the semicircle of gravel before the house, and left it at the front door. He went into the hall and stopped immediately to look at the messages. He was reading them when a door opened and his mother said:

'I have some tea all ready. You have time for a cup before you do anything else.'

He walked to join her and kissed her cheek.

'Hallo, Mama. . . . I'd better pop along and see old Mrs.

Williams, they think she's had another attack.'

'Not now, Ivor.' His mother spoke with determination. 'You at least have time to sit down and have a cup of tea.' She saw him glance at his watch. 'Oh yes, you can have tea and still see Mrs. Williams before surgery. I insist.'

He went into the cheerful living-room with her. She poured his tea immediately, and he stood at the window holding his cup, looking out at the lake.

'Oh, do sit down,' she said impatiently. 'The world won't come to an end if you take five minutes off.'

'Somebody could die in five minutes.' But he smiled as he said it and sat down in an armchair near her own. 'Old Mrs. Williams, for instance. That was a nasty attack she had this morning, and if she has had another, I think it must be the end. By the way, your friend Hilda became a grandmother this afternoon – her daughter had a nice seven-pound baby.'

This satisfactorily diverted his mother's thoughts from old Mrs. Williams and provided more cheerful conversation for the short time Ivor allowed himself to stay.

'Well, off again,' he said, rising to his feet. 'I'll go straight to surgery from the Williamses. Hope to be back about seven-thirty.'

They both knew that he would be lucky to get back to supper by eight, luckier still if there were no calls to make after it. His mother watched him go. It seemed that this had been her whole life, sending the doctor out, trying to keep meals hot against his unpredictable return. First her husband, then both husband and son for the few years they were in practice together, now her son.

As he went out to his car, the telephone rang. Mrs. Huwlett went to answer it, but Ivor had heard it and came back into the house. He waited until his mother rang off.

'The Tompson child. Cut himself with the carving knife.

His mother says blood all over the place. It's Rose Terrace, those dismal little houses near the warehouse.'

'Right, that'll be first, then. 'Bye, Mother.'

The car shot off. The four-year-old Tompson boy was not nearly so bad as the amount of blood indicated. He was soon bandaged and his arm put into an important-looking sling, and his mother given a talking-to about leaving carving knives where children could get at them, which she was too distraught at the moment to heed. Then he went to Mrs. Williams, who was just holding her own after the morning's heart attack.

The cottage was so small that he wondered how she could have raised a family in it. Now there were only her husband and herself, living more comfortably on the old-age pension than they ever had in the old days. The house was spotless. Mrs. Williams was now a ghost of an old lady bearing her suffering patiently upstairs. The arrival of the doctor was a great relief to them both: they had known father and son for many years and their trust was implicit.

Ivor Huwlett left tablets for the wife, a sedative for the husband and promised to call in the morning.

'Have a cup of tea, doctor,' said the old man, slowly seeing the doctor downstairs. Ivor did not want tea (everybody in this area seemed to drink tea all day long), nor had he time for it, but the old man wanted a few minutes' reassurance. So he put down his bag, went into the diminutive kitchen, and waited as patiently as he could while the tea was made, talking to comfort the old man.

He was a few minutes late for surgery, going in by the waiting-room to see what it held for him this evening. Hmm, a fair number. There was a murmur of 'Good evening', 'Evening, doctor', and one woman spoke up, asking if he had been to see Mrs. Williams.

'Yes, just come from there,' he said.

'How is she, doctor?'

'Well, you can't expect too much at her age,' he said, and they knew what he meant. She'd been Granny Williams to them all for so long, and they were sorry for the old man, and they had something to talk about as the doctor went on into the surgery and began the evening's work.

It was ten past eight when he returned home.

'You didn't wait for me, did you?' he asked his mother.

'Of course I waited for you. Would you like to eat right away?'

'I'd like to sit down for five minutes first,' he said. 'What about a drink? I nearly stopped at the Greyhound for one, and then thought I'd come and have it with you.'

'Good. I'll get it.' He sank down into a chair and Mrs. Huwlett brought his Scotch and water and poured sherry for herself, and they relaxed in their chairs. She knew he would enjoy his meal more for this short respite, and hoped that the ringing of the telephone would not shatter this moment of peace, nor the supper to follow it.

'This is more pleasant than the Greyhound,' Ivor said, looking round the room softly lit by wall lights and an elegant white-shaded table lamp, furnished with the good pieces his parents had been able to afford in the later years of the long practice.

'Strange about the Greyhound,' concurred his mother. 'I'm sure they try as hard as the people at the Tudor Rose; but the Greyhound can't seem to put a foot right, and everything the Tudor Rose does is a success. When you urgently need a reviver, you must try the Tudor Rose.'

'What about the long family feud? I might get thrown out.'

'It always was a nonsense,' declared Ginette Huwlett. 'Your father and I were always prepared to patch it up.'

'Well, you weren't the ones who suffered, were you?' her

son reminded her. 'You weren't the ones to forgive, you had to be forgiven. Can't you just imagine the shock, the hurt pride, etcetera? After all, Miss Knight – what is her name now? oh yes, Catherine – Miss Catherine Knight was engaged to Dad, and there were only two weeks before the wedding, so I suppose she had everything ready for it; wedding dress, all the fal-lals, bridesmaids and *their* fal-lals, reception arranged, *this* house arranged for her to move into: then, pow! Back he comes with a bride, and only a letter to the poor forsaken fiancée. I really don't know how you could have done it.'

'*I* didn't do it, Ivor, and well you know it. It was entirely your father's doing. He didn't say anything to me about being engaged, almost married. He simply clapped eyes on me, fell in love like a stone and dragged me off to marry me …'

'You couldn't have been unwilling.'

'Naturally. I took one look at him and knew he was the man I'd been waiting for all my life. We fell in love and we never fell out. … And if I'd known about Catherine Knight, it wouldn't have made any difference; but I'd have tried to arrange it all in a more seemly manner; so that, somehow, she could have saved her pride if nothing else.'

'As it was, they just cut off all communication.'

'And have done to this day,' said his mother. 'Come along, Ivor, supper.' They walked together into the dining-room, and as they seated themselves, she went on: 'They immediately changed their doctor, of course. And your father never again went to the Tudor Rose. They ignored each other if they happened to meet in church, and people around never invited the two families to the same parties, so there it was, the feud persisted, even widened.'

She was serving the meal from her much-prized electric wagon, which kept food hot without spoiling it.

'But it's mad to allow a feud to last so long,' said Ivor.

'Agreed, but it's hardly a feud any longer, it's just a state of affairs. For the Knights, the Huwletts don't exist, and vice versa.'

'They obviously exist for you, since you seem to like talking about them. I believe you still have a guilty conscience. Anyway, the Tudor Rose has a new receptionist today, and she's a beauty.'

'How do *you* know?'

'I found a maiden all forlorn standing on the pavement with a mountain of luggage, so I offered her a lift, and she was making for the Tudor Rose to work there. I imagine the clientele going up by leaps and bounds. Blonde hair, and a skin like peaches and cream.'

'Well, well, well,' said his mother, looking at him in astonishment. Ivor smiled.

'Don't look so surprised. *I* haven't fallen like a stone. It's just that there aren't so many complexions around here like peaches and cream.'

'There might be if you looked for them.'

'I don't have the time. Most of the complexions I see are ailing ones, pale or worn or with spots on them. . . .' The telephone bell shrilled in the hall. Ivor looked at his mother and she looked back at him. 'I'll answer it,' she said. 'You're just going to finish your supper. If it's necessary, I shall say you'll be with them as soon as possible.'

Lake Mereworthy was a recognized beauty spot. Its shores had been saved from the jerry-builder until the middle of the century because they belonged to large estates; and since then they formed part of a national park on which it was almost impossible to get planning permission to build.

It was, however, one of the less frequented beauty spots.

15

For three months of the year it was comparatively busy. Cars huddled at awkward angles in inconvenient places while their occupants picnicked by the lake, parties of young people in a vari-coloured assortment of strange dress hiked over the hills, older couples with walking sticks went more sedately over them. Rowing boats motionless on the lake held fishermen almost as immobile. The Tudor Rose was always full, and non-residents wishing to lunch or dine there were advised to book beforehand to avoid disappointment.

During the other nine months of the year, it was a quiet place. It was for the quietness that early and late visitors came to the Tudor Rose, congratulating themselves on having found such a comfortable spot with such congenial people.

Lately, however, changes were taking place in the area around Mereworthy Lake. There had always been the Village, south-west of the lake, with its people almost entirely dependent on the mine; and the Town, north-east of the lake, with its weekly market, catering for the more prosperous farming community living on the richer lands. They had very little to do with each other. Only a bus service connected them, and that was a poor one.

The Village was dying. The pit had been closed and the miners had to go further afield to work, often having to change their homes to do so; which, in spite of the poverty and cramped conditions of those mean terraced houses, they were very reluctant to do. This took away the able-bodied and their children, and left behind the less able-bodied, the old, the widowed.

The authorities had tried to bring light industry to the area, but this effort had backfired; for the people brought in to work it and run it were of a different kind. They wanted bright new houses on new developments. They drove to the

Town to shop. They liked to drive out to the Tudor Rose for the occasional dinner, or more often only for the drink after dinner, in one of its cosy bars. All of this was good for the Tudor Rose, which had never drawn its custom from the Village. Mr. and Mrs. Knight felt that they could make a success of a much larger place, and had long-cherished plans for one.

For the doctor it made life more complicated. He had always had a special feeling for the people of the Village, a special relationship with them. They had trusted and relied upon his father, approved of the son working with him, and already had an allegiance to the young man when the father died. They said he was a good doctor without realizing just how good he was. They were at home with him, in many cases he seemed like an extension of the family.

With the new people, there was a different relationship. Everything was more impersonal. There was not yet room for a group practice, but Dr. Huwlett felt that many of them would approve of one. Dr. Pasture practised in the town, but Dr. Pasture was getting old, and some said, neglectful and forgetful too. Since his wife's death a year or two ago, he increasingly sought solace from his whisky decanter. It was time he took a partner. Meanwhile, more and more patients came to the surgery at the side of Dr. Huwlett's house at those times when he was not taking surgery in the Village.

He was overworked, and knew it, but was still young enough at thirty-five, and tough enough, not to be afraid of overwork – even, in fact, to enjoy it.

This was how things stood at the time that Gabrielle Knight returned to work at the Tudor Rose. For her family, prosperous and smoothly-running. On those spring mornings, when she woke to cool sunshine playing on the lake, flowers blooming in the hotel courtyard, the smell of bacon and new bread faintly drifting to her through the hotel, it was good to be alive.

On one of those heart-lifting spring mornings, she went riding. Colonel Reid-Browne, who kept several horses in the stable attached to his handsome house a mile or so from the Tudor Rose, had said he would be grateful to her if she would exercise them from time to time. Gabrielle, recognizing the generosity of this, was delighted to oblige him.

Usually she rode on the hills, where she could get an exhilarating gallop; but this morning she took a narrow side road which she believed led up to old quarry workings. She remembered, as a child, running up to the old quarry with two boy cousins and two girl school friends who were spending holidays with her. All the way up, as the road twisted and turned, there were beautiful views, the lake seeming to get bluer the higher she went.

The road had certainly deteriorated. She doubted if it had been repaired at all since those childhood days. The quarry had long ceased working, and she supposed that few people ever came this way now.

She rode through a wood, and coming out to the uplands, turned a sharp bend in the road to find herself confronted by a Land-Rover. She reined in suddenly. The man in the Land-Rover stopped with a screaming of brakes. They came to a standstill within inches of each other.

Dr. Huwlett had been coasting silently down, carefully avoiding ruts and boulders. He found himself once more looking at blonde hair shining in the spring sunlight. It was a few seconds later before she recognized him.

'What are you doing up *here*?' she called out, astonished to meet him in this forsaken spot.

'I might ask you that,' he said. He had stepped out into the freshness of the morning. 'Why aren't you working?'

'Oh, you know what hotels are like. Very irregular hours.

I was working until half past ten last night. But what possessed *you* to bring a car up here? It doesn't go anywhere.'

'It goes to the old quarry.'

'Are you prospecting, then? I don't think you'll find gold among all that slate.'

'There is also a line of old cottages.'

'But nobody lives there.'

'Nobody *should* live there, not even a dog. But two of them are occupied. Not officially, I might say. Squatters.'

'You're not going to buy the cottages, are you?'

'Heaven forbid!' He looked about him with sudden awareness, as if emerging from another world. 'Not even for *this* view,' he said.

'You refuse to satisfy my curiosity,' she said. 'And quite right. Why should you?'

He turned his eyes from the spectacular view to look at her.

'I'm sorry,' he said. 'I didn't realize you were curious. I've been doing an appendectomy on a boy. Which had been ignored until almost too late. Too late to get him to a hospital anyway.'

'Oh,' she said, on a long-drawn-out sound. 'You're a doctor?'

'Yes.'

'A surgeon, I should have said.'

'A doctor will do. I'm a qualified surgeon, and I get plenty to do in a scattered practice like this; but I work as a plain old G.P.'

'I have an idea you're not a plain old G.P. at all,' she said. She knew now who he was. He couldn't be old Dr. Pasture. He could only be Dr. Ivor Huwlett, and she had already heard quite a lot about *him*. 'How is the boy?' she asked.

'He'll live.' After a moment or two he felt he had been impolite. 'He'll be all right now. He could do with something better than the stale bread and tea he'll get there. I wish I'd thought to bring something up with me. . . . Well now, I have work waiting for me. Tell me first, how are you making out?'

'As you predicted,' she told him with a smile (which she had no idea was as dazzling as it was), 'I'm enjoying my work at the Tudor Rose.'

'Nice people?' he asked her casually. She looked at him with slight suspicion. Had he found out, too, who *she* was?

'Very nice,' she told him.

'Good.' He was getting back into the Land-Rover. 'Enjoy your ride, he said. 'Good-bye.'

She watched him as he coasted down into the wood and disappeared. So that was Ivor Huwlett! He was the son of the man who had treated her aunt so disgracefully, so shabbily. Not his fault, of course, except that he was, after all, his father's son.

She remembered seeing him when he was a young man and she only a child. He was twelve years older than she was, and so their paths had not crossed. They must sometimes have been at the same function – party or garden party or fête – but if they had been, they would still have been in different age groups: and since boarding school, she had been mostly abroad, at finishing school, and working in many different hotels. Strange to think that his father and her Aunt Catherine had once been intimately close; that Aunt Catherine had looked forward to living in the house at the other end of the lake, where he, Ivor Huwlett, had been brought up.

'What a shabby trick to play on any woman,' thought Gabrielle, imagining it happening to herself, still watching the spot where he had disappeared into the woodland.

Then, admitting to the curiosity which drove her on, she

continued her way up the hillside to the old quarry, and to the line of tumbledown cottages where it did not seem possible that families could still live. One or two of them were beyond all hope, the slates of the roof disappeared, rafters exposed to the sky and inside ceilings gone, or hanging by one corner. It was obvious which were the two still occupied. Two ragged children were playing happily among scattered boulders and Gabrielle stopped to speak to them.

'Does the road go much further?' she asked them, although she seemed to remember that it stopped right there.

They stared at her wordlessly, shocked into shy silence. A woman appeared suspiciously in one of the doorways to see what she wanted. Gabrielle smiled at her.

'Does the road go much further?' she asked politely.

'It don't go nowhere,' said the woman. 'It stops here.'

'Thank you.' There was a short pause. 'Is it your little boy who just had an operation?' she asked.

'Why do *you* want to know?' The woman was still suspicious, thinking perhaps that Gabrielle had something to do with the dread world of officialdom.

'I just met the doctor and he was talking to me about it.'

'Oh. Dr. Huwlett.' The suspicion disappeared. 'Yes, that's my boy. We might 'a lost 'im, but for Dr. Huwlett. There's a kind man for you.' She saw one of the children poised perilously on a huge boulder that rocked slightly. 'Come orf that!' she shouted, her softer mood immediately dispelled. Gabrielle thought it wise to leave, and began to pick her way carefully among boulders and down the hill.

When she returned to the hotel, having left her mount with Colonel Reid-Browne, she went to the yard at the back where the small van, which picked up supplies, was being cleaned by Jim, the handyman.

'Do you know the old quarry up in the hills, Jim?'

'Sure. Played there often when I was a boy.'

'Would this van get up there all right, do you think?'

'Should think so. Bit rough going at the top. Why?'

'I wanted to send up some stuff to people living in one of the cottages there.'

'Go on! Nobody lives there now.'

'Not officially perhaps, but a boy up there had an appendicitis operation this morning, and as the family seems to be on its beam ends, I'd like to send up something.'

'O.K., Miss Gay. I can manage that this afternoon.'

'No need to say where it came from, Jim.'

'O.K., then. Mum's the word. You just let me have the stuff.'

Mrs. Sanders, up in the old quarry, was astounded to receive a parcel of food so rich that she was almost afraid to give it to the children. It was the plainest, most sensible food Gabrielle could find, but for the Sanders it was luxury. And Mrs. Sanders had no doubt where this manna came from. Only Dr. Huwlett would be likely to have such a kind thought as that.

CHAPTER TWO

THERE was a road on only one side of Mereworthy Lake, although on the other side there were many tracks for walking, and a large car park concealed by trees. The road, running the whole length of the lake, kept to the shore almost all the way. The exception, where it had to make a considerable detour, was where the Medlicott estate occupied what was undoubtedly the most beautiful part of the whole district.

Medlicott House had been built in the middle of the nineteenth century, but old Mr. Medlicott had had his own ideas, steadfastly refused Victorian Gothic, and had built a stone house with mullioned windows which had mellowed well and looked more beautiful today than when it was built. He had set his face against lofty ceilings and Victorian ideas of grandeur, although, when it came to the outside and the garden, he had given way and indulged himself with a wide terrace running the length of the house, and a noble flight of stone steps widening out at the bottom on to a green sward that swept down to the lake. He had planted trees and shrubs that were now magnificent; including rhodondendrons and azaleas which people came long distances to see in the spring, when the gardens were open to the public.

This was when Mr. and Mrs. Knight and Aunt Catherine indulged their dream of one day turning Medlicott House into a hotel. There was little likelihood, but one never knew! and in these days of ruinous death duties anything might happen. They could imagine the tables and chairs set out on the terrace, where people would have tea in the afternoon, drinks in the early evening; could see guests strolling down those wide steps towards the water.... No more than a dream – at present.

When Gabrielle returned from her travels to work at home, there were three Misses Medlicott living at Medlicott House, granddaughters of the house's founder. They had lived the most uneventful lives it was possible to imagine. None had married or been engaged or had a love affair. Only two years separated Mabel and Etty, but Ivy, who had been her parents' afterthought, was twelve years younger than Etty, still only forty-eight, although a strangely elderly forty-eight. This was no doubt due to the three sisters being such constant companions, and age rubbing off the elder ones on to the younger.

Gabrielle knew them slightly, for they issued forth from Medlicott House in their old but resplendent Rolls-Royce to have dinner at the Tudor Rose a few times each year. They also made occasional trips to London where they stayed in a Kensington hotel, shopped mainly at Harrod's and imagined they were keeping abreast of affairs. Gabrielle as a child had thought them old: they had always seemed old, but Miss Ivy was certainly the liveliest of the three. They lived so secluded a life that people had almost forgotten them, and newcomers were unaware of their existence.

So that when the bolt fell, few people were concerned, and among those few, perhaps the Knights were the most.

Gabrielle and Aunt Catherine were in the small room behind the reception desk when Mr. and Mrs. Knight came in in a hurry, obviously with news to tell.

'Whatever's happened?' asked Catherine, seeing the suppressed excitement.

'Something almost incredible,' said Mrs. Knight. 'Miss Mabel and Miss Etty Medlicott have died.'

'No!' there was a stunned pause. 'Good heavens, how did that happen?'

'Well, we knew they'd gone to London . . .'

'A road accident?'

'No. Much more improbable than that. Nobody knows *exactly*, apparently. We met Major Craddock, who had it from Dr. Pasture, who had been called in by the cook to see Miss Ivy – who, of course, is prostrated. It seems they died of gas poisoning. The hotel people smelled the gas and went into their room and found them both dead . . .'

'They're sure it was an accident,' went on Mr. Knight. 'They think they wanted to light the gas fire – it's one of these old-fashioned but very respectable hotels – and then couldn't find any matches and forgot to turn off the gas.'

'They'd been quite lively, showing the manageress patterns of curtains for the drawing-room at Medlicott. Quite *forward*-looking . . .'

'How is it that Ivy wasn't with them?' asked Catherine.

'She had had 'flu, and was feeling below par. Even if she had gone, she wouldn't have been in the same room. The older sisters always shared. I imagine it's been a dreadful shock for her.'

'They've always been so close to each other.'

Gabrielle left them, to fetch coffee. She knew what this meant for them. She knew that this opened up a prospect which they would not look at as yet, because it seemed heartless in the face of somebody else's suffering.

Those poor old sisters, she thought. Not so old, really. No older than her father, nor quite so old as Catherine; but seeming years older. Elderly in thought and fashion and their style of living, whereas her father and aunt were busy and lively and kept pace with the times.

Poor Miss Ivy! She could hardly live in that great mausoleum alone. It had been much too large for the three sisters, half the house shut up and never used, the servants reduced to a cook, a housemaid and a chauffeur-gardener. Ivy, alone, could only be a hermit there. Gabrielle, knowing the ideas taking wild flight in her parents' minds, could not help feeling an enormous sympathy for the remaining sister and wondering what she would do.

What Miss Ivy Medlicott was *not* doing, at that time or for some time after, was facing the future. It seemed to her that she had no future without her sisters, almost no separate being. It would have been a blow almost past bearing to have lost one sister, leaving a great gap in the lives of the other two; but to lose both sisters at once was more than she could bear. She took to her bed and Dr. Pasture gave her a sedative and promised to return that evening.

He did not return. A telephone call to his surgery elicited the information that Dr. Pasture himself was not well.

'Not well,' said the cook to the chauffeur-gardener with scorn. 'We all know what *that* means.'

'There's no relying on him these days,' the man agreed.

Neither of them felt competent to shoulder the unpleasant tasks of the immediate future. The only living relative of Miss Ivy was her aunt of over eighty living comfortably in a private nursing home. She would be a hindrance more than a help and not be disturbed.

'I shall send for Dr. Huwlett,' said the cook.

So Ivor Huwlett entered the impressive stone doorway of Medlicott House, took charge of Miss Ivy with sympathetic understanding, realized that she was in no condition to face her problems – the return of her sisters, the funeral, the decisions about the future – and settled down to help her face and solve them, starting by contacting her solicitor.

Other people sent sympathy, and went to the church for the funeral service; the vicar's wife spared what time she could from her young family; Mrs. Knight called to offer sympathy and help (and had every intention of calling again); but it was Dr. Huwlett who captured Miss Med-

26

licott's complete confidence, so that she vowed she would never have that drunken Dr. Pasture again.

'I don't want to poach on another doctor's preserves,' Ivor told her.

'It's time he retired,' Miss Medlicott declared. 'Several times he has come here smelling most strongly of whisky. At least, he should take a partner. You are not poaching, Dr. Huwlett; in any case, as a private patient, I can choose my doctor.'

'Very well, Miss Medlicott. When you need me, I will come; but I think you don't need me any longer just now.'

She quickly banished the panic that had shown momentarily on her face. Ivor thought she was fundamentally a sensible person, but for the moment quite lost.

'Miss Medlicott,' he said gently, 'I don't want to intrude on your private life, but surely you aren't contemplating living in this great house alone? That can't be good for you.'

'I don't know *what* to do at the moment, Dr. Huwlett. There is so much to be done. My sisters' wills have to be proved. My solicitor advises me not to stay – he suggests a smaller house, or even a flat. But how can I leave this beautiful place? All my life has been spent here. My sisters and I have always loved it, have always thought how *lucky* we were to be able to live here.' Her eyes filled with tears at the thought of her sisters. 'I don't think I *could* bear to be anywhere else.'

Ivor looked out of the drawing-room window, across the terrace and the green sward sweeping down to the lake, and thought: 'God, yes, she's been lucky, she doesn't know *how* lucky.' He thought of old Mrs. Williams, still hanging on to life in great suffering in that tiny bedroom which could scarcely accommodate the double bed. He thought of the squatter's family up in the hills; and of old Mrs. Goodall, too grossly fat through illness to get out of the house, relegated by her daughter-in-law to a small back room, which looked out at a yard and a stone wall.

In that moment, the idea was born. He turned from the enchanting view and looked at Miss Medlicott, wondering how kindly and humane she was, how soon he could plant a small seed, how receptive the soil would be. He said:

'You could always live in a part of it, Miss Medlicott, and put the rest to some good use.'

This idea apparently struck her as a very strange one. Before it had sunk in, or Ivor had time to say more, the maid appeared with a small silver tray bearing two glasses of sherry and a plate of biscuits. Had Ivor but known, this was a signal honour. It was a rite the three sisters had shared at this time of the morning, and now Miss Medlicott's eyes filled with tears as she remembered.

'You must forgive me,' she said. 'I shall never grow accustomed to their absence.'

Ivor pressed the pursuance of his idea.

'You must find other things to fill the gap,' he said gently. Then: 'This is very good sherry, Miss Medlicott: if I may, I shall call in and see you when I'm passing, to keep an eye on you and drink another glass with you.'

'That would be splendid. As often as you can.'

'I'm a busy man.'

'I know, I know. One hears about you. But I am your patient too, Dr. Huwlett. And I do appreciate this wonderful offer of friendship.'

He thought that was enough for one day. But he had no intention of letting the grass grow beneath his feet. He could hardly wait for the next occasion. The sherry finished, he said he would see himself out and left her in her drawing-room; but as he went through the big hall, he looked about him with an interested and practical eye, and felt a stirring of excitement at what he might be able to persuade her to do.

At the end of the drive, he had to get out to open the gates. He drove through and was closing them again, when he saw a horse and rider approaching along the road through the dappled light and shade of the trees that added to Miss Medlicott's privacy; and guessing who the rider was, waited for her.

'Good morning,' she called to him as she drew near.

'What a pleasant existence,' he said. 'And what a nice job you must have, always riding round the countryside.'

'I assure you I do sometimes work quite hard. Have you been to see Miss Medlicott? How is she?'

'Well, naturally, she's shocked and upset and very ready to collapse. The three sisters were exceptionally close. Because they had each other, they didn't need to look outside for friends ...'

'I wonder what she intends to do. Surely she won't go on living in that big house all alone? She *would* be lonely then.'

'Her solicitors have advised her to sell,' he said, 'but I think it's too early yet for her to have decided anything.' He was back at the door of his car. 'I must get on,' he said. 'I wish I had the time at my disposal to come riding with you. You look as fresh as the morning, without a care in the world. It's a tonic to look at you. I wish all the people I'm going to see today looked as beautiful.'

Gabrielle was surprised.

'I didn't think you noticed people unless they were ill,' she said, giving him her sunny smile.

'It would be difficult not to notice *you*,' he said, gave her a wave of the hand and got into his car. Gabrielle moved her horse up beside him.

'You must have an hour some time when you could ride,'

she said. 'Colonel Reid-Browne would be delighted to lend you a mount. You think about it.' She moved away to let him drive on.

She watched him go, following on at a walking pace. She was back at the Tudor Rose in time for lunch, and as they seated themselves, she told her family what she had learned.

'*If* she decides to sell,' said Mrs. Knight, 'we must get in first with our offer. It would make such a marvellous superior hotel.'

'I can't see her ever leaving,' said Aunt Catherine.

'But don't you see,' exclaimed Mrs. Knight, 'she needn't leave! She could have her own apartment in the hotel. Absolved of all responsibility, looked after, excellent meals regularly served; and her own garden to wander in, her own lovely views – and added to that, company into the bargain.'

'It sounds ideal,' her husband agreed. 'What are the snags?'

'Perhaps she wouldn't like other people tramping all over her house,' said Gabrielle.

'Half of it is shut up already. It will get gloomier and gloomier if she stays on alone. If she sells, she can at least go on living there. And *we* get our hotel.'

'I'll call on her this very afternoon,' said Mrs. Knight. 'Oh, of course, I'll be tactful, but I can keep my eyes and ears open . . .'

They felt a stirring of excitement at the possibility of getting Medlicott House into their hands, precisely as Ivor Huwlett had done earlier in the day. Two plans of campaign were about to be born.

Mrs. Knight called at Medlicott House and was offered tea; admired the view so much that she was asked to walk out on the terrace, and invited to come again when the rhododendrons and azaleas would be out. She told Miss Medlicott that her daughter Gabrielle would like to call on her, if it would not be too much at the present time, and was invited to send her along for sherry next morning.

'Do go, Gay,' her mother said, when she was at home again. 'You must see the house. The drawing-room would make a perfect lounge, and I saw a morning-room which would make a television room. I didn't see the dining-room, but I expect it's huge. The whole place just cried out to be a hotel. A very exclusive sort of hotel at that. And of course that terrace, and the wide steps leading down, and the lawns and grounds!'

It was obvious that her mother had set her heart on the place. Catherine, filling dishes for the hors d'oeuvres trolley, said:

'Don't you go building this up, Pamela. You might be in for a big disappointment. You've no reason to think it's coming up for sale.'

'If it doesn't, I shall have to plant the idea in her mind. Gay, if there's a chance for you to do that, you do it.'

'Don't involve the child,' grumbled Catherine; but Gabrielle was inclined to believe, with her mother, that it might be all for Miss Medlicott's good.

She went for sherry next morning and was struck by the forlorn loneliness of her hostess. They walked down to the lake together, where daffodils were flowering in great masses, and Gabrielle stayed longer than she had intended to. She was invited to go again, and in fact visited Miss Medlicott three times that week, her mother only too willing to give her time off, if it furthered her own cause.

The third time, as they returned from a short walk in the grounds towards the grand flight of steps and the terrace, Gabrielle said:

31

'It really is a lovely house, Miss Medlicott.'

'But so much, much too big for me now, alas.'

'It *is* big,' Gabrielle agreed.

'My solicitor says I should sell, but it goes against the grain. The gardener has a very good cottage, but I could not possibly turn Hillyer out after all these years, nor would the place be at all suitable. There is also the coachhouse. My solicitor thought that would convert into a nice, small house, but somehow I cannot face the work involved. And who would want to buy such a big house?'

'Plenty of people still do.' Gabrielle hesitated a moment, then added quickly: 'It would, for instance, make a super hotel.'

'Oh, do you think so?' Miss Medlicott was surprised.

'Yes.' There ensued a long silence. Gabrielle waited for a reaction to her idea. Miss Medlicott was remembering Ivor Huwlett's suggestion that she could live in a part of the house and use the rest for some good purpose. They walked slowly up the steps together and Miss Medlicott paused on the terrace and stood looking around her. She was silent for so long that Gabrielle decided she should take her leave, and was about to say good-bye when Miss Medlicott spoke:

'If it became a hotel,' she said slowly, 'there would be no reason why I should not live in it myself.' There was another pause. 'I could choose my rooms. That would be possible, wouldn't it?' she asked Gabrielle.

'Of course,' said Gabrielle. 'What a good idea! As you say, the house is much too big for you, but that would give you what you want, and take away what you don't want.'

'And I wouldn't have to go away. I must think about it. My solicitors thought it could be a private school – a finishing school perhaps. But I couldn't live in a finishing school . . .'

Gabrielle drove home feeling she had achieved something

for her mother. She reported the conversation verbatim and her mother clapped her hands in her excitement.

'Oh, we must follow it up,' she cried. 'We mustn't let anybody else get in first. I was thinking about the big entrance hall, how reception could be at one side and a really super bar at the other . . .' She was off again, airing plans that had been forming in her mind for a long time. The rest of the family begged her not to count her chickens but to keep in mind that her plans might come to nothing.

Gabrielle, whenever she rode or drove out, kept an eye open for Dr. Huwlett. The words he had spoken to her would not be erased from her thoughts. 'Fresh as the morning. Not a care in the world. A tonic to look at you.' And: 'It would be difficult not to notice *you*.' She did not think he was a man who spoke his words lightly; and if he felt that, why should they not go riding together? She went as far as to ask Colonel Reid-Browne if he would lend a horse to a friend of hers, and armed with his willingness, she telephoned Ivor Huwlett on Saturday evening.

A woman's voice answered her.

'Dr. Huwlett is out on a case,' it said. 'Will you leave a message?'

It was rather a forbidding voice. Gabrielle could not be expected to know that the doctor had been called out three evenings running immediately after his supper. She said apologetically:

'Well, if you wouldn't mind asking him to ring up the Tudor Rose . . .'

'The Tudor Rose?' That *did* surprise the person at the other end of the line. 'You said the Tudor Rose?'

'Yes.'

'Very well. I'll give him the message.'

'Thank you,' said Gabrielle. 'Good-bye.' But the person at the other end had already cut off.

Gabrielle was in the hotel dining-room, helping a party to select from the somewhat exotic menu, when Ivor rang back; she hurried out to speak to him, explaining that, if he had a free hour, she had a mount for him for the following morning.

'Well . . .' He made it a long-drawn-out sound.

'Don't be so enthusiastic,' she said, rather snappily.

'Let me think,' he said. 'I've just delivered twins. Quite long and complicated. I'm almost as tired and woolly-brained as the mother . . . I believe I have things to do in the morning. Just a moment. please.' Gabrielle held the line for a minute. 'It's all right,' he said. 'I'd like to ride in the morning, if you will let me kill two birds with one stone.'

'Meaning that you want to call somewhere?'

'Two somewheres. Will that be all right?'

'I see that I have to take a back seat,' she said.

'I'm sorry.'

'No, *I'm* sorry. I do understand really. And I'm sure you're tired. Are the twins all right?'

'Very big and bouncing and bonny. That was what caused the trouble. What time in the morning? . . . Fine, that will give me time for leisurely eggs and bacon.'

Each time she had seen him, he had worn a practical fine tweed suit and immaculate shirt and tie. For riding, he wore breeches, a thick, polo-necked sweater and a ridiculous woollen hat with a bobble on it. She had arranged to meet him at Miss Medlicott's driveway. She was riding a chestnut mare and leading a big bay.

He brought his medical bag out of the car and started to fix it to the back of his saddle.

'You aren't going to wear that ridiculous thing, are you?' she asked, looking at the woollen hat.

'Don't you like it?' He took it off and slung it into his car. 'I'm attached to it myself. Never mind,' The wind at once

34

began to blow his dark brown hair. 'I hope this animal is good-tempered,' he said as he mounted.

'Where are we going?' she asked him.

'To the northern end of the lake and up into the hills a little way. A farm, where the son of the house has a crushed leg. A tractor ran away with him and crushed him against a tree. He's just out of hospital. Then, if we've time, to see an old couple in a tied cottage on another farm.'

'Let's go, then,' said Gabrielle.

The morning was superb – clear, sunny and fresh. The bird-song was incredible, continuous, liquid and varied. 'This is a heavenly place for bird-song,' she said. They jogged along together, in silence at first, then speaking intermittently of nothing very important. They were able to take a short cut over fields to the farm, and had a comfortable trot; and once at the farm, Gabrielle too was invited inside for coffee and 'a nip of something'. They all sat in the big kitchen, where Sunday midday dinner was cooking; with the back door open so that fresh breezes came in to them. When they went on, they were in a heightened mood, exhilarated.

'Is it far to the cottage?' asked Gabrielle.

'About a mile. Pushed for time?'

She looked at her watch.

'Mmm, no. Only I have to be back for Sunday lunch. Busy time, you know. Weekenders.'

He nodded. They jogged along towards the cottage, the air fresh on their faces.

'I won't be long,' he said. No question of asking her in here. An old couple, he had said, both frail.

'I'll ride around,' she said, 'and lead Robin Adair.'

She went up the road into the woods and came back to find that the doctor had not yet emerged. She cut off along a farm track, until she thought he must be waiting for her, and hurried back to find that he had still not come out of the cottage. 'Drinking tea, I suppose,' she thought angrily. 'And he knew I was in a hurry.' After her years on the Continent, she could not accustom herself to the local passion for drinking tea. Her watch told her that she was going to be late. She almost went up to the door to knock on it and find out what was keeping him. Some element of respect for his doctoring restrained her. She fumed in impatience. She thought of going away without him. She could leave Robin Adair tied up for him, and he would have to return him to Colonel Reid-Browne himself.

'Oh *lord*,' she exclaimed, frustrated, angry, 'what the blazes can he be doing in there?' She rode a short way up the road, back again, up again, back again. 'Well, I'm going,' she decided at last, and was in the act of tying up Robin Adair when at last the door of the cottage opened, and Ivor Huwlett came down the long path carrying his bag.

'What on earth kept you so long?' she demanded. 'I'm going to be hopelessly late.'

'I'm sorry,' he said.

'I should think so. You said you wouldn't be long. You've been hours. Drinking tea, for a certainty.'

'Yes,' he said quietly. 'Drinking tea.'

'Well, you might have had more consideration,' she said angrily. 'Let's get going, for pity's sake.'

'What are you so angry about?' he asked.

'Who wouldn't be angry, kept waiting while you sit drinking tea? You knew I hadn't much time.'

'Will it lose you your job?' he asked.

'No, of course it won't lose me my job. Oh, let's get going. It's the inconsideration that makes me so angry.'

Now he was angry too. He mounted, but turned Robin Adair so that she could not get past him, and looked her straight in the eye.

'Let's hope you never have more cause than that to be angry,' he said. 'A man in there has died. He died this morning.' He was speaking quickly, in a clipped voice. 'There's a poor woman in there, nearly eighty, not well herself, with the dead body of the man she's been married to for nearly sixty years, a man she had six children with. She didn't only need someone to sign the death certificate, and advise her about the undertaker, and promise to send telegrams to her married sons and tell her married daughter in the Village. She needed somebody to talk to, somebody to hold her hand, to make her a cup of tea. She wanted somebody to hear what a good husband he'd been to her all these years.' He paused. He wasn't looking at Gabrielle now, but across the fields away from her. 'I'm sorry I kept you waiting,' he said in a quieter voice. 'Weekenders waiting for a good Sunday lunch just don't seem as important to me.' He swung his horse round and they began to clip-clop along the lane. 'You see that trying to kill two birds with one stone is not a success,' he said. 'It's no good trying to mix business with pleasure.'

Gabrielle was utterly silent. He had put her completely in the wrong, by, it seemed to her, an unfair advantage. She could not say she was sorry. The words stuck in her throat. They rode in silence, trotting where they could; but when they reached the Tudor Rose, she would not go in, but insisted upon going to where his car was, and taking back both horses.

'Thank you,' he said drily.

'You're welcome.' Her tone matched his. 'Good-bye.' She turned and did not look back. Ivor started his car and went in the opposite direction. He drove past his own house, because he had to tell the dead man's daughter that her mother was alone up there in that tied cottage. It was still some time before *he* would sit down to his Sunday lunch.

A few days later, he called on Miss Medlicott and found her considerably livelier and brighter. He drank the customary sherry with her, but observed that she no longer deserved his attention as a patient.

'I hope you won't stop coming on that account,' Miss Medlicott said. 'It's true that I've been trying not to dwell on the past, but to consider plans for my future, and the future of this house.'

He was immediately alert.

'Have you decided what you are going to do?'

'No, not yet. It's early days, and there is still a great deal of business to be done by my solicitors. But at least I have been given food for thought: in fact presented with an idea which would make it possible for me to stay here, while using the rest of the house as well.'

'What is this idea, Miss Medlicott, and who presented it to you?'

'It was that nice Knight family, who run the Tudor Rose. Mrs. Knight was very kind in calling on me and so was her daughter. *They* think, and Mr. Knight agrees with them, that this house would make a wonderful hotel; and they hope that, if I decide to use it other than as a private dwelling, I will allow them to make me an offer . . .'

He gave an exclamation of annoyance.

'A hotel!' he exclaimed impatiently, and was so patently put out that Miss Medlicott regarded him with surprise.

'But you yourself, Dr. Huwlett, advised me to do something of the sort. You said I could live in a part and use the rest for some good purpose.'

'Some *good* purpose, yes.'

'And you don't think a hotel is a good purpose? It would mean that I could live here, and at the same time give other people a great deal of pleasure.'

'No, I don't think a hotel is a particularly good purpose. I had something rather different in mind.'

'For this house?' She was still surprised.

'Yes.'

'So you had designs on it too,' she said quietly. There was a pause. 'How extraordinary! The Knights at one end of the lake tell me they have wanted it for years as a hotel. You, at the other end, have apparently wanted it for something else.' There was a sadness in her voice that told him she was thinking of the peaceful years in it with her sisters, when she had no knowledge that others wanted it in their clutches.

'I know,' he said. 'It sounds rather like the vultures gathering. But I had never thought of your house in any connection whatever, until you sent for me. *You* planted the idea in my mind when you said your solicitor advised you to take a smaller house. I believe that was when I said you could stay here and use some of the house for a good purpose.'

'Yes, that was so.'

'Before that, Dr. Pasture was your doctor. I don't believe I ever set foot in the house, though I knew the grounds from your Open Days. So I can safely say I never harboured plans for it.'

'And what plan are you harbouring now?'

'I think it would divide up splendidly into flats for old people. In my work, Miss Medlicott, I come across old people who are perishing from loneliness. Not only poor people, though God knows there are enough of them; but old men or women, left alone, not wanted by their families, who have enough money to live in comfort but no friends. *They* can be lonely without privation, though loneliness is loneliness wherever it is found. The really poor ones have privation too. . . . I could give you instances, case after case, where a word to the milkman is looked forward to eagerly; or any sort of excuse engineered to keep the meals-on-wheels lady for just a moment longer. As for the doctor, he is fair game – and he mustn't cast them off.'

'I can see,' she said slowly, 'that this is something very dear to your heart.'

He would not have put it quite so romantically, but he agreed that it did mean a lot to him.

'What a pity that I have almost said the Knights may have the first refusal.'

'Almost said?' he repeated. 'What does that mean? That isn't binding. It's what *you* think, Miss Medlicott, that matters. What *you* wish to do with your own property. It's the Knights who are the vultures . . .'

Miss Medlicott surprised him by laughing with genuine humour at those words.

'Dear Dr. Huwlett, you are losing your sense of proportion. Who could call Mrs. Knight, so young-looking and pretty, a vulture? Or that quite beautiful daughter? Why shouldn't they have plans dear to their heart as well as you?'

'The daughter?' he asked, remembering only now that the Knights had a daughter who had been abroad for some time. Abroad? In Switzerland, Italy, France, for instance? A daughter who was golden-haired, with a complexion like peaches and cream? But he remembered the daughter as a gangly schoolgirl. He said: 'I thought the daughter was abroad.'

'She came back just lately to work in the hotel,' Miss Medlicott told him. 'A charming girl.'

'Fair hair? Very nice figure? Good complexion?'

'Yes, that's her – Gabrielle Knight.'

Gabrielle Knight. On the first three occasions, they had been strangers briefly meeting and parting. On the fourth, riding together, he had meant to ask her name. It was amazing that it hadn't been mentioned.

Gabrielle Knight. Not only was she 'on the other side' as a member of a family that had no use for the Huwletts: she was also there as one of a family who wanted Medlicott House for a hotel, while he wanted it for something he considered much more worthy.

CHAPTER THREE

It was Sunday afternoon, of one of the two Sundays that the grounds of Medlicott House were open to the public. Cars were parked along the whole length of the drive and filled the coachhouse yard. The sun turned the blossom of rhododendron and azalea into a brilliant splendour, and many people from both Town and Village were strolling over the lawns, beneath the shrubs and by the lake. The Azalea Walk was a great favourite, a wide path of velvety grass bordered on each side by subtle colouring from ground level back to a great height. The swans on the lake were clustered near the shore where people fed them continuous titbits.

Miss Medlicott stood in the drawing-room, back from the window, and looked at the scene. She could not quench the sadness that filled her because this was the first time her sisters had not been here to witness it. Last year it had rained on both the Sundays, few people had come and very little money had been raised for charity. The sisters had implemented the amount themselves. So beautiful today; they would have enjoyed being here today.

Suddenly, among a sea of anonymous faces, she recognized Dr. Huwlett walking with a woman who could only be his mother. Miss Medlicott decided to go and meet them.

Ivor Huwlett had not wanted to go. 'I've seen the rhododendrons and azaleas there several times already,' he reminded his mother. 'Then come as my escort, darling,' she said, and he had agreed. They greeted Miss Medlicott with pleasure and they were enjoying an enthusiastic conversation about gardens when the Knights came into view.

There were four of them, Mr. and Mrs. Knight, Catherine and Gabrielle. They were lost in admiration of the towering rhododendrons and had not yet seen the Huwletts. When they did, their instinct was to turn away, but Miss Medlicott was beaming upon them and beckoning to them to come closer, so they advanced somewhat warily.

'You do all know each other, I'm sure,' said Miss Medlicott warmly. They looked at each other, suspicion mixed with curiosity, and on the part of the Knights with a definite coldness. Mrs. Huwlett thought that the daughter was indeed attractive, with a beautiful figure and wonderful colouring; but Catherine Knight had aged, and did little to counteract the years.

Catherine, on the other hand, was intensely annoyed by Mrs. Huwlett's elegance and poise. 'Soignée,' she thought. She had always been soignée. Groomed to the hilt, elegant as a ballet dancer, with a grace that made Catherine Knight feel clumsy. Her dislike took on a sharper edge, a new focal point, as she contemplated the elegance of Mrs. Huwlett.

These elder people were so full of suddenly revived old feelings that they did not notice Gabrielle and the doctor. She was looking at him uncertainly, for they had parted on any but amicable terms; and he was returning her look with a detached curiosity that annoyed her. For he was wondering why she had chosen to hide her identity when she must certainly know his, what was the reason behind it.

Miss Medlicott became aware of a coldness and reserve where before there had been cordiality. She tried to restore the warmth by inviting them all in to tea. Mrs. Knight immediately accepted, prepared to improve any shining occasion. It was Mrs. Huwlett who gracefully and tactfully slid out, saying that the doctor had an appointment.

The Knights followed Miss Medlicott into the house. Mrs. Knight had only one idea in her head – to approach the subject of the new hotel; but the elderly maid appeared just then with the tea trolley. When she withdrew, it was Miss Medlicott herself who made it easy.

'I don't believe you have ever been over this house, Mrs. Knight.'

'No. We've always admired it very much from the outside.'

'It would be a pleasure to me to show you. You may well decide, when you have seen it, that it wouldn't suit your purpose at all.'

'Oh, I feel sure that it would; and I would certainly like to see it.'

'You see, I think I should tell you that somebody else is interested too. Not as a hotel, for quite a different purpose; and as I say, *you* may find it unsuitable, after all.'

Mrs. Knight looked at her sharply. Her first thought was that this was a way of telling them they need not expect to get the house too cheaply because there was a rival (real or imaginary) in the field. Then she decided that this was not so, and the thought that a rival might in fact exist frightened her and filled her with a real anxiety.

'Would it be an impertinence to ask what this other person wants it for?' asked Gabrielle in a clear voice, thus exhibiting a courage that her mother had not risen to.

'Not at all. *He* knows that you want it for a hotel. I don't see why you shouldn't know that he wants to convert it into flats for old people.'

'Flats for old people!' It was a shock to Mrs. Knight.

'Flats for old people,' echoed Gabrielle – and saw the light. 'I suppose it's Dr. Huwlett,' she said, stating a fact more than asking a question. Miss Medlicott agreed that it was Dr. Huwlett.

'The Huwletts again!' exclaimed Catherine angrily. She could not forget the quiet elegance of Mrs. Huwlett. She

44

was reminded of all the humiliations she had suffered at the hands of the Huwletts. Miss Medlicott, recognizing the bitterness in her voice, suddenly remembered, rather vaguely, some trouble between the families. She said:

'Yes, well, it's all a little difficult. But anyway, come and see the house.'

They had a comprehensive tour. And they found it perfect for their purpose and told Miss Medlicott so. Back at the Tudor Rose, their annoyance and anxiety found voice.

They were in their private sitting-room. Mr. Knight poured sherry and passed the glasses round.

'I couldn't bear to lose it now,' said Mrs. Knight, 'knowing the possibility really existed.'

'I didn't even know he was her doctor,' said Catherine.

'He wasn't, until Dr. Pasture was too fuddled to go out to her and the cook called him in,' said Gabrielle.

'And of course, once he got a toe in the door, there would be no keeping him out,' said Mrs. Knight.

'Like father, like son,' said Catherine.

'In his persistence, do you mean?' asked Gabrielle.

'In his unscrupulousness,' retorted her aunt sharply.

'But how has he been unscrupulous? He has simply said he saw a use for the house. Are we unscrupulous because we want it for a hotel?'

'He would just like to put a spoke in our wheel.'

'Oh, nonsense, Aunt Catherine.'

'*You* don't know what that family is like, Gabrielle.'

Gabrielle did not answer. She might not know the family but she thought she knew Ivor Huwlett better than her aunt did. She saw him astride Robin Adair, looking at her with a steely glint in his eyes, putting her firmly in her place, letting her know what *his* priorities were. She saw him in imagination in that small cottage making a cup of tea for an old lady suddenly bereft of her lifetime partner. She thought of the poverty-stricken family up in the old quarry cottage and of Ivor Huwlett operating there, probably on an old kitchen table which had had to be scrubbed thoroughly beforehand. These were but two of the dozens of tasks he did daily. No, she could never believe he was unscrupulous; though she might accuse him of self-righteousness, in believing that his world was the only one worth while.

Her family was still discussing the latest events, but Gabrielle left them to return to the reception desk, where Mary had been taking her place.

'The Flannagans arrived about half an hour ago, Miss Gay,' Mary told her. 'They'll be in to dinner. The Arkwrights rang up to say they will arrive late, and could they have something cold when they get here?'

'Thanks, Mary. Anything else?'

'Only old Miss Frobisher. She wants to change her room because the cars leaving at night when the bars close disturb her.'

'Yes, I'll see to that.' Mary left, and after a few minutes Catherine joined Gabrielle from the small room behind the desk. Unnecessarily, she rearranged the flowers at one end of the counter, emptied an ash tray, flicked through the letters still in the letter rack.

'Gay, I do hope nothing is going to prevent your mother and father getting their hotel,' Catherine said suddenly and earnestly. 'I couldn't bear them to be done out of it by the Huwletts. We've been overshadowed by them most of our lives.'

'Oh, Aunt Catherine,' Gabrielle protested. 'You know that isn't true. For years on end, they've probably hardly thought about them.'

'Well, I have,' her aunt said bitterly.

Gabrielle looked at her, wondering whether to speak or not. Then, courageously, she said:

46

'Even you, Aunt Catherine, have been happy here in this house.'

'What do *you* know about it, Gay? How can *you* say whether I've been happy? For years you've been abroad. Before that you were a schoolgirl. You understand nothing. Do you think it's pleasant to intrude on one's brother's private life, living with him and his wife all through the years; when, but for that Huwlett woman, I would have had my own husband, my own house and my own life? Yes, and perhaps my own family too.'

'Aunt Catherine, I'm sorry.'

'So I should think,' was the sharp retort. 'There was not much likelihood of marrying anybody else then, either; with almost a generation of young men wiped out by the war. And it's the years after the *first* war I'm talking about. No, when Anthony Huwlett married Ginette Roderer, he put paid to my chances, and he did it in a completely unforgivable way.' She was silent, looking back to those far-off days; and when she spoke again, it was in a quieter voice, reminiscing.

'It was two weeks before the wedding when I had his letter. We had spent months buying furniture for the house, and I was always there supervising the decorating. We had chosen wallpapers and curtains together, and had received dozens of wedding presents. I had my wedding dress and the bridesmaids had theirs, and we were going to Cornwall for the honeymoon. There wasn't so much going abroad in those days. And then one of my friends mentioned that Anthony was back from London and I thought it odd that he hadn't come to see me; and she said there was a woman with him, and I naturally thought it was somebody who was coming to our wedding. But it was his wife! I had his letter next day, telling me so.

'All my friends were so sorry for me. I couldn't bear to

put my head out of doors. Knowing that *she* was using the furniture I had chosen, living in rooms decorated to my taste; and I was left with a useless wedding dress and a mountain of shame. Don't talk to me about the Huwletts, I've had my cross to bear on their account; and I just hope that a Huwlett doesn't score over the Knight family again.'

Gabrielle was astonished by the amount of heat still in that family feud after so long a time; but she had the perspicacity to realize that today's meeting had revived it. Suddenly, she saw that it might well have been a strain on Aunt Catherine all those years to live with her brother and his wife, even though she was working for them; perhaps a strain on her mother and father too, who had certainly never shown any signs of it to Gabrielle.

She saw too that as far as she was concerned, her loyalties could not be divided. She knew that her family, but particularly her mother, would realize a long-cherished ambition by running a large and beautiful hotel superbly well. She could not have sympathy for the other side, lest those loyalties should begin to be divided.

She was now a regular visitor to Medlicott House. She and Miss Medlicott had taken a liking to each other, and Gabrielle was welcome there any morning for a glass of sherry, any afternoon for a cup of tea. If Gabrielle went riding, she would call in for a few minutes, feeling that she was probably furthering her mother's cause by winning Miss Medlicott's friendship.

One morning, as she rode along the drive towards the house, she met the doctor's car approaching her from it. She stopped in the middle of the driveway so that he could not pass her, and almost before she realized that the words were in her mind, she had called out:

'Have you been putting in some useful spade work?'

The car window was down, or he might not have heard her. He waited for her to ride alongside before he said:

'What is that supposed to mean?'

'I think you know, Dr. Huwlett. Winning friends and influencing people . . .'

'Which you, of course, would be too lofty to consider doing.'

'Well, I hardly think Miss Medlicott needs your services as a doctor any longer.'

'But perhaps she needs friends.'

'Unself-seeking friends.'

'Do you call yourself that?' he asked.

'Yes, indeed.'

'Good,' he said, his voice detached. 'That's just what she needs. But I don't think you're yet in a position to censor her other friendships, Miss Knight.' He switched on the car engine. 'Now as my job makes more demands on my time than yours seems to do, I must get along. Good-bye.'

'It doesn't stop you coming here!' she called after him as he started off. Sanctimonious prig! she added in her mind. A doctor was a doctor. All right. And some doctors were dedicated. That didn't give them the right to act as if nobody else's job was worth doing. She dug her heels into Chestnut's side with unnecessary sharpness and rode on to the house, considerably ruffled.

It might have interested her to follow his course that morning.

Ivor was less ruffled by the brief exchange. True, he was going to try to influence Miss Medlicott, and he had no doubt that the Knights would too. Eventually, only Miss Medlicott could decide the outcome. As he drove away, he thought Gabrielle Knight looked beautiful with the wild colour in her cheeks that riding had given her; but he saw her now as her loving parents' spoiled daughter, who indeed

49

might have a job with them but who need not work if she preferred to ride.

His mind had no time to dwell further on her. He was bound for a cottage in the Village where a girl had tried to commit suicide. She had been rescued from herself, had spent several days in hospital and was now at home again, from where she would attend a psychiatric unit as an out-patient.

Ivor Huwlett had an uncomfortable feeling that he had failed the girl. She had been a patient, but for no specific illness. She had been 'fed up', had cried a great deal, had complained of headaches, sore throat, various pains which came and went; but he could never find anything wrong with her. Now, as he drove towards her home, he wondered how her life could be rearranged to keep her this side of breakdown.

She was unresponsive as ever, but she trusted the doctor. Old Dr. Huwlett had delivered her. Young Dr. Huwlett had treated her ever since his father's death.

'What's getting you down, Deirdre?'

'I don't know.'

'Are you in any pain?'

'No.'

'Just fed-up?'

'Yes.'

'Not all the time?'

'Mostly all the time.'

She sat collapsed into a heap, playing with the bandages round her cut wrists. The doctor had already satisfied himself that she was not pregnant.

'Got a boy-friend?' he asked her.

She shook her head.

'Ever had one, Deirdre?' Perhaps there had been a break-up in her young life.

50

She shook her head again. Perhaps she needed one.
'Girl friends?'

'Well . . .' She shrugged her shoulders. 'Sometimes. One or two.'

'Get on with them all right?'

'They're all right, I suppose.'

'You get on with your mum and dad?'

'All right, I suppose.'

'And what about your job? Like it there?'

She shrugged helpless shoulders.

'Let's see, it was the dress factory, wasn't it?'

'Mmm.'

'Well, how do you get on with the girls there?'

'I'm a machinist. They keep you at it. Too noisy to talk.'

'Does the noise get you down?'

'I don't know. Don't think so.'

So it went on. Almost impossible to draw a reaction from her. Out of a mass of question and answer, he must find the thread that would connect with her trouble; or she would attempt suicide again some time – and next time perhaps with more efficiency. He felt a responsibility for her.

Next he went to change the dressing on a man's wounded arm, cleaning the pus out carefully, securing the new dressing: a time-consuming task and for the patient a painful one. He said: 'Well, doctor, I could do with a nip of brandy after that. What about you?'

Ivor smiled.

'I'd like to, but I'd better not. I'm off to see a real old tartar, and if she smelled brandy about me she'd probably report me to the B.M.A. But thanks.'

He set off for the elderly woman, pretty sure she was a malingerer, but until he was sure he would not neglect her.

Since this kind of routine was no isolated one, but of everyday occurrence, he had little time to think about Gabrielle Knight. Even at lunch time, when he ate alone since his mother did not eat in the middle of the day, he read the leading medical journals, joining her afterwards for coffee.

Gabrielle, however, thought a good deal about the doctor, always with a slight discomfort, a touch of annoyance. Her job at the Tudor Rose was child's play to her. Her work in a large international Zurich hotel had kept her busy all through the day, and she had needed her several languages. Here, in this less than busy season, she had more time to herself than would be possible later on, and plenty of time for thinking. And she was coming to the conclusion that the doctor was humane and sensitive in his treatment of his patients, somewhat less than human to anybody who was not one.

This conclusion was put to the test the next time they came together. It was a late evening in early May. It had been a day of exceptionally heavy rain, and now that the rain had stopped, white mist had descended from the hill tops to envelop the valley, shifting uneasily, breaking now and then for short distances of clearness: a heavy, humid, dangerous evening, with the sides of the roads lying under water, which sprang into fountains with every passing car.

Ivor Huwlett was enjoying a brandy in his living-room, a reading lamp beside him, the baleful telephone silent for the moment. (Gabrielle, miles away, was saying good-bye to friends with whom she had had dinner, and stepping into her car for the drive home.)

When the telephone did ring shrilly from the hall, Ivor said: 'It was too good to be true,' and went to answer it. An agitated voice said there had been a car accident and a man was trapped beneath a car and would the doctor come at once.

He asked for the precise whereabouts of the car and put a few pertinent questions. He looked round the living-room door to say to his mother: 'Looks like a serious accident along the lake road,' and then hurried to his dispensary for blood plasma. On the gravel sweep outside the house, the Land-Rover was waiting, the stretcher already inside it. He drove with as much speed as was possible through the misty night, saw ahead of him a cluster of lights, and drew in to the side of the road.

A police car was already there. A constable came to the side of the Land-Rover and when Ivor wound down his window, said:

'Pass along, please, sir. There's been an accident and we don't want a crowd of sightseers.'

'I'm the doctor. Where's the man?'

'He's down there, sir. The car overturned on the bend, demolished the bollards, must have thrown the man clear and then toppled on top of him.'

Ivor could now hear where the man was. His screams of pain quieted the few people standing round. He scrambled down the slope to the overturned car.

'Only one person in the car?' he asked the constable.

'No, there was a lady too. She was thrown clear and seems all right. But for shock, of course.'

Ivor now had no attention for the constable.

'All right, old man,' he said to his patient. 'All right now, I'm the doctor.'

The morphine was injected immediately, and as if in anticipation of the relief he soon would have, the man was not so hopeless. 'Can you give me more light?' Ivor asked one of the policemen, and their car was turned so that its light beamed over the scene. The doctor was setting up the plasma for a transfusion.

It was this curiously lighted scene that Gabrielle saw as

she rounded the bend. She also saw the doctor's Land-Rover; and although it was not her custom to stop at the scene of accidents, she stopped now, pulling her car in behind the Land-Rover. The constable was at her side, asking her to pass along, please. 'We don't want sightseers here.'

'You already have quite a few,' she remarked.

'These gentlemen were witnesses of the accident. The lady was thrown out of the car. Pass along, please.'

'Dr. Huwlett can do with my help,' she said; and she said it with such confidence that he thought she must at least be a nurse, and let her stay. She stepped out and looked at Ivor and the wounded man and the people standing around.

The morphine had worked. The man's eyes had closed. Relief spread through all the watchers who had heard his cries of pain. Their thoughts could now turn to other things.

'Came round that bend like a streak of lightning,' said one man.

'Didn't have a hope of getting round,' said another.

They were two of four men who had been in another car going in the opposite direction. They had seen the whole thing. They remembered a parked police car and went back to notify the accident. Already, the police had sent for an ambulance which should soon be here.

Gabrielle scrambled down the slope, stopping at Ivor's side. 'Is there anything I can do?' she asked him.

He gave her the briefest possible glance, identifying her.

'Go and look after the poor woman,' he said. 'Give her some brandy which you'll find in my car. Keep her warm.'

She went at once. At the top of the slope, she looked back. He was instructing those witnesses how to shift the car so that he could get at the man's injuries. 'I must at least set the arm and the leg,' he said. They all heaved in the soggy mud at the bottom of the slope, the police helping. Gabrielle saw that the doctor gave them no more attention. Once the car was lifted enough, he left it to them to arrange it so that he could work; and down there, in the mud, under the over-hanging car, he got on with his work as calmly as if he had been in an operating theatre.

He was the man in authority. Everybody accepted that. They did exactly as he said. Gabrielle, too, who had fetched the brandy from the Land-Rover and helped the distraught wife of the injured man into her own car, persuading her to take a drink, wrapping a rug round her. Even while she did her best to comfort the woman, her eyes refused to leave that compelling scene below: alternate brilliance and deep black night, with wisps of mist drifting across the headlights. She heard Ivor asking: 'Is there anybody to bring the stretcher from my car?' and the constable who was waving on the passing traffic came to the Land-Rover for it and took it down to him.

At last the ambulance appeared, and the men were down there with the doctor, knowing exactly how to interpret his instructions, and the man was carried up carefully and placed in the ambulance.

Ivor came to the side of Gabrielle's car.

'You'll want to go with him?' he said to the woman.

She nodded helplessly. Tears were streaming down her cheeks. Ivor opened the door for her, helping her out.

'Don't give way,' he said, gentle, yet matter-of-fact. 'He's got a chance. You've got to keep up for his sake.'

She went in the ambulance with her husband. Ivor stood, using the side of the ambulance as a desk, to write a note to the hospital surgeon. The ambulance driver took it, and they were off to the distant hospital.

The police were taking the names of the witnesses. Ivor said:

'You don't want me any more?'

'No, doctor, thank you. We know where to find you.'

'O.K. Good night, then.'

'Good night, sir.' There was a chorus of respectful good nights. Gabrielle knew how they were feeling, because she felt the same herself. Respect and gratitude for the man, whoever he was, who could command such a bad situation, who knew what to do. He had worked with a calm sureness, single-purposed.

But now he looked worn and his face seemed all hollows. He stood at the side of Gabrielle's car, and he said:

'God, I'm tired.'

'Get in,' she said. 'I'll drive you home.'

'A tempting offer; but what about the Land-Rover?'

She thought for a moment.

'The police will bring it back for you. I'll fix it. You get in.'

'I've got about four pounds of mud on each foot,' he said.

'Never mind,' said Gabrielle. She went to speak to the policemen. In a moment or two she was back.

'They'll follow with your Land-Rover as soon as they've finished writing in their little books,' she said, and she smiled at him. 'You do look done up,' she said sympathetically.

'I'd already had a pretty heavy day,' he said in explanation; and he slid down in his seat and rested his head on the back of it and closed his eyes. Gabrielle drove steadily along the lake road through the drifting patches of mist and when she came to the doctor's house, turned on to the gravel sweep and switched off the headlights.

'Here we are,' she said, wondering if he had fallen asleep.

He had not. He pulled himself up in the seat flexing his shoulders and turned to face her; at the moment that she let her hands drop from the driving wheel and turned towards him. In an almost unconscious reflex action, they drew together, and his head was against her shoulder and her cheek rested on his hair. She felt the deep sigh he gave, felt his weight heavy upon her and stayed breathlessly still.

It lasted only a few moments. He moved very slightly away. They could see each other dimly in the subdued light that came from the hall windows; and in the shadowy car there was a feeling of waiting, of slight suspense, for what was going to happen. A moment that might have been magic, but it was put to rout, banished for ever, when a brilliant headlight lit them up garishly from behind.

'The police,' said Gabrielle.

'They've been quick,' replied Ivor, and opened his door to go and thank the police. One parked his Land-Rover for him, then joined the other in the police car. Gabrielle did not wait for them to finish talking. She started her car, turned it, and pausing briefly by the men, said:

'Good night. I'm off home now.'

'Good night, and thank you,' said Ivor. The policemen saluted her and she left them behind on the driveway, making her way back to the Tudor Rose, her mind over-full of all that had happened since she saw the cluster of lights about the accident. She could not think tonight, as she had thought at their last meeting, that he was a sanctimonious prig. Nothing, tonight, could be farther from the truth.

A few days later Gabrielle was busy in her office. Several people were leaving that morning and she was making up bills, speeding travellers on their way, typing letters for her father. In buckets on the floor, out of sight of the reception desk, she had masses of cut flowers ready to assemble into beautiful arrangements for the entrance hall, lounge and dining-room. Her mother brought in mid-morning coffee for herself and Gabrielle.

'You can take the afternoon off if you'd like to, Gay. It's a lovely day and you might as well make the most of it. Things are going to hot up here at the weekend.' (Which would be Whitsun.)

'What about you? Why don't *you* take the afternoon off?'

'Yes, I will, one day this week. Or one evening. You can have today. Why don't you go in and see how Miss Medlicott is?'

'Oh, you wretch, you're just using me! You're dying to know if she's thought any more about the house.'

'Of course I am. I wouldn't be in this indecent haste but for that busybody Dr. Huwlett pushing his oar in. I could afford to wait, before I knew about him.'

'All right, Mama, I'll see what I can find out.'

After lunch, Gabrielle drove away from the Tudor Rose, wearing a crisp little yellow suit which made her look part of the spring day itself. The drive of Medlicott House was still beautiful with blooming rhododendrons. As Gabrielle stopped her car before the main door, she saw the doctor's car waiting there; not the Land-Rover he used for difficult climbs into the hills, or for accidents when he might need his stretcher. Briefly she considered going away and coming back later: then decided she would like to see what his attitude to Miss Medlicott was, and went and rang the door-bell.

The housemaid, Susan, now well into middle age, opened the door and smiled at her.

'Good afternoon, Miss Knight.' She opened the door wider and Gabrielle stepped in. 'Will you come this way? Miss Medlicott is in the garden room.'

It was a very cosy scene which met Gabrielle's eyes in the garden room. The sun streaming in through the tall glass panes made the room very warm, and there was a profusion of growing plants in colourful bloom. On each side of a low coffee table with the coffee tray still on it, Miss Medlicott and Dr. Huwlett sat in comfortable chairs. They had the air of people interrupted in absorbing conversation. Dr. Huwlett stood up, offering Gabrielle his chair.

'My dear, how very nice to see you,' said Miss Medlicott. 'Come and join us.'

Gabrielle took the chair the doctor offered. She said:

'*Not* one of your heavy days, Dr. Huwlett,' and wondered at once why it was he always provoked her to sarcasm.

'Even *I* have an occasional day off,' he said, pulling up another chair.

'Will you have some coffee, Gabrielle? No? Then you may take the tray, Susan.' Miss Medlicott turned back to Gabrielle. 'I think it is very kind of Dr. Huwlett to spend part of his free day lunching with me. It has been extremely interesting.'

Gabrielle could imagine.She had never known Ivor Huwlett to expand in conversation – he was always brief with her – but she guessed that he might indeed be stimulating when he was on a subject dear to him. Such as converting a house as beautiful as this one into flats for old people! She would have liked to be a fly on the wall during that 'extremely interesting' luncheon, feeling that whatever they had talked about would not be to the benefit of the Knights.

After a while, Ivor Huwlett rose to his feet.

'I must be off now, and thank you for such a pleasant time. We shall look forward to seeing you for dinner next Monday.'

'I shall look forward to that too. Do thank your mother for me. Gabrielle dear, you will excuse me, won't you? I am going to call on my solicitor this afternoon.'

Gabrielle rose too. She was not going to find out anything this afternoon.

'Come and see me again soon,' said Miss Medlicott.

'I'm going to be very busy, I'm afraid, with Whitsun looming up.'

'Come before then – tomorrow perhaps? and have some tea.'

Gabrielle said she would be delighted, and went out with Ivor Huwlett. They stood together on the drive, the air wonderfully fresh on their faces. He took a deep breath of it.

'Wonderful to be alive,' said Gabrielle.

'Yes,' he said. He thought to himself: For some people – and then was struck by another thought. He said:

'You're having a day off, too.'

'A half day, in anticipation of a busy time.'

'Would you like to spend it with me?'

Gabrielle glanced at him, aware of a quickening in his voice.

'Doing what?' she asked him.

'Driving here and there,' he said casually. 'A mystery tour for you. Something I'd like you to see. Are you game?'

'I feel there's a catch in it,' she said suspiciously.

He laughed.

'A challenge,' he said. 'Are you going to accept it?'

She hesitated only briefly, knowing she could not resist. 'Yes,' she said.

'We'll leave your car here then, and go in mine.'

It was pure coincidence that it should have been such a glorious day when Ivor went to lunch with Miss Medlicott and Gabrielle's mother had the idea of sending her there too. As they set off together in Ivor's car the countryside around them was green and gold and even the air seemed to be impregnated with gold. The blossoming spring. On every

60

hand, masses of flowers in cottage gardens, orchards foaming with the white of cherry and the scarlet tips of unfurled apple blossom. When they left the low land and climbed up through the woods, dappled sunlight flickered and sparkled through the fresh green of the leaves, and when they came up out of the woods on to the uplands, they had unimpeded views of the hills and the sky: a blue sky with billows of white cloud moved across it by the fresh breeze.

Ivor drew his car off the road and stopped it near the edge of a precipice.

'There, isn't that worth coming up for?' he asked, waving a hand at the view.

'But that isn't a challenge,' commented Gabrielle, 'or what you brought me up for.'

'Wouldn't it be enough?' He turned his face towards her and she saw a sparkle in his dark eyes. Suddenly, even as she returned his regard warily, she thought what a nice face he had: a bit craggy, hollows here and there, no longer a young and untouched face. Indeed, moulded by his experience. But interesting, attractive.

'Yes,' she said, 'it would be enough, it's quite lovely, and I already know it very well. I think you brought me up for something else.'

'Yes, I did. Don't get alarmed, though.'

'I'm not alarmed.'

'Because I'm so trustworthy, or because I'm dull?'

'How do I know you are trustworthy? Or how do I know that you are *not* dull?' asked Gabrielle, determined to give as good as she got. 'If we're going somewhere, let's go.'

He started the car and they went on up the twisting, narrow road, stopping finally at a small cottage standing at the foot of a rugged cliff and almost enclosed by stunted trees.

Ivor opened the car door for her.

'I come too, do I?' asked Gabrielle.

'You come too.'

Their knock on the door was answered by a little old woman whose back was permanently bent.

'Oh, doctor,' she said with obvious delight. 'Come in, come in.'

'This is Miss Knight, who is interested in my work. Miss Knight, Mrs. Barnes. I called in to see how you're getting on, as I was up this way.'

'I'm keeping pretty well, doctor. Only the old complaints, you know, and I suppose they're with me for ever. Now you're going to have a cup of tea with me, aren't you?'

'We'd like that,' he said. 'Can we come and help you?'

'You know you always do just as you please in this house, doctor.' So they went out into the tiny kitchen, not very well equipped but beautifully clean, with crisply starched gingham curtains at the window and the inevitable few geraniums. The almost as small living-room was as clean and well cared for; and there were home-made buns on the tea tray.

They stayed with her for half an hour, and she was delighted. Her problem was loneliness. Oh, she managed, she said: very well, in fact. The postman brought her milk and bread, bless him, even when he didn't have to come up this far. Of course, he didn't have to bike any more, they had those nice little red vans. She had other ways of managing too, but she couldn't get out any more, except for a short doddle round her patch of garden when the sun shone.

Gabrielle began to get the idea, but said nothing about it. They went from Mrs. Barnes to a semi-detached cottage on a farm, where lived an elderly man who suffered from pernicious anaemia and needed weekly jabs. Gabrielle waited in one room while the jab was given in another, and they stayed for a short time here too. *His* problem was also lone-liness more than illness. 'My son would have me any time,' he said to Ivor. 'He's always saying to me: "Come to us, Dad, we'll look after you". But you should see *her* face when he says it. Sour as a quince! A nice life I'd have if I ever took him up on it and went to live there. My son out at work all day, and me stuck in the house with her! That'd put me in my grave fast enough . . .'

Gabrielle was very quiet as they went back to the car. 'Don't let their problems depress you,' Ivor said kindly. 'They always spill them out on the doctor.'

'Well, where do we go now?' she asked. Her voice was a little dry, detached. Ivor did not seem to notice it.

'If it won't bore you, just one more call,' he said. 'Does it bore you, Miss Knight?'

'No, it doesn't bore me, doctor, and please don't go on calling me Miss Knight. My name is Gabrielle, or if you prefer it, Gay.'

'I like Gabrielle,' he said. 'And don't call me doctor. *My* name is Ivor.'

'I know,' she said.

The third house was different from the other two. The only common factor was its remoteness from town or vil-lage. And here lived Mrs. Gresham, a lady every bit as gracious as Mrs. Barnes but considerably better off. Her living-room was full of treasures, but her house was full of sad memories. Her husband had recently died, they had had no children, but had lived for each other. She obviously thought her own life no longer worth living; and the doctor considered that as long as she stayed in that house, she would be constantly reminded of her sorrow.

They accepted tea there too, China tea from fragile cups. Yes, thought Gabrielle, loneliness is the problem here too; and she saw what was behind Ivor's desire to spend the afternoon with her.

'What endless cups of tea you drink,' was her only comment as they set off in the car once more.

'I used to hate the stuff. I've learned to like it. Most of them only do it because they want to keep me a bit longer.'

They were making their way back to pick up Gabrielle's car. She did not want to talk and refused to make conversation. He too seemed to be sunk deep in thought. They came to Medlicott House and both got out of the car.

'I hope you had a pleasant afternoon,' he said, looking down at her with some concern.

'Why did you ask me to go with you?' Her question was direct and her voice not entirely friendly.

He continued to look at her, and a ghost of a smile was present on his face and in his voice as he replied:

'Oh, I thought you might well have a soul to save.'

Her reaction to this remark was completely unexpected. It was undeniable that a wave of anger had swept through her.

'How damned superior!' she said, and repeated it: 'How damned superior!' She had difficulty in restraining all she would have liked to say to him. She opened the door of her car, and then turned her face back to him, still angry. 'Just how priggish and sanctimonious can you get?' she asked, and got into the driving seat and slammed the door of her car shut.

Ivor did not move. The surprise on his face changed to comprehension. He wanted to go to her side, but would not allow himself. He had an impulse to say to her: 'It was a joke' but thought that, when she had recovered herself, she would realize that. He watched her drive away without a backward glance, and only then did he move to get into his own car.

CHAPTER FOUR

'MISS KNIGHT,' they said, 'do you think we could have four packed lunches. We thought we'd go for a picnic today.'

'Certainly,' said Gabrielle. 'We *do* like to know before you are ready to go out – by breakfast time, if possible.'

'We only just decided, because it's such a lovely day.'

Gabrielle gave the order to the kitchen and turned back to her accounts.

'Miss Knight,' somebody else said, 'do we have time to go to the Castle and have a good look round, and come back in time for lunch?'

'By car?' asked Gabrielle. 'Oh yes, then you have plenty of time.'

'Which is the most attractive route?'

This meant picking out the road for them on their map, and they went off, all smiles.

'Miss Knight, excuse me, have you stamps for letters going abroad?'

It was the Whitsun holiday and this sort of thing went on all the time. Non-residents asking anxiously: 'Can we have morning coffee here, please?' and Gabrielle's pleasant voice directing them to the lounge and sending a waiter to them. Residents with complaints, who had to be soothed. People coming in for accommodation – quite hopelessly, since the Tudor Rose was always completely booked for Whitsun well ahead.

Then a deep, pleasant masculine voice said:

'Good morning. I wonder if you have a single room available.'

Gabrielle looked up from her typewriter, stood up and

came towards the counter. She saw a tall, broad, handsome man, deeply tanned, whose eyes were dark blue and whose smile was devastating. She responded to an overpowering charm and smiled back ruefully, shaking her head.

'We're quite full up, I'm afraid.' There was a pause, during which he hoped she would think of something. 'How long did you want to stay?' she asked.

'A week.'

'We have a room for tomorrow night, when some of the weekenders leave; and I could give you a better room after that. But for tonight . . .' She spread her hands in denial.

'Do you know of anywhere else,' he asked, 'that might have a room?' He saw opposite him a girl neither tall nor short, slim yet still delightfully curved, with glorious golden hair and a skin one would like to touch.

'There's the Greyhound at the other end of the lake,' she said. 'But I should think that's full too. Would you like me to ring them for you?'

'Do you recommend it?' he asked.

She hesitated.

'You don't,' he said. 'I can see that, so don't bother to ring them.'

'There's a very nice cottage on the first lane to the left. A Mrs. Thomas who does bed and breakfast. You could go and see her; and we could give you meals here.'

'I'll do that,' he said. 'Will you book me in for tomorrow night, and for lunch and dinner in the meantime?'

He arrived for lunch, reporting to Gabrielle at her desk in passing that Mrs. Thomas could put him up for the night. 'And you'll put up with me for the rest of the week?'

'We'll be delighted to do that,' she said.

She had no time off that day. Everybody working in the hotel was busy. Mrs. Knight went to help her husband and the usual barman in the bar. She and her husband had always kept Gabrielle out of the bars: there was plenty for her to do without that. During lunch and dinner, on those busy days of Whitsun, she was present in the dining-room, with an ear alert for the ringing of the bell on her reception counter. She knew that diners were very impatient until their order was taken. They then felt that something was on the way. She took orders, offering suggestions, explaining certain items; and she saw to it that the rolls arrived promptly so that if customers had to wait a little time for their food, they had something to nibble. She tried to get the wine waiter to them promptly. She removed empty dishes from tables that looked crowded, and even removed the used plates at the end of a course to help the hard-worked waiters and waitresses.

The newcomer, Howard Nelmes, found her the most pleasant thing to watch in the dining-room. She, on her side, while appearing not to notice it, was very well aware of his admiring attention. At the end of his meal, she went across to remove his cheese plate.

'Coffee?' she asked him.

'Please. Black.'

'In the lounge, or the saloon bar? Or here, if you prefer.'

He decided on the saloon bar, which was in fact an extremely pleasant room, close-carpeted, well furnished with chairs and tables, with the bar at one end. 'Would you care to join me there for a drink?' he asked her.

She shook her head, smiling at him.

'I'm looking forward to my dinner,' she said, 'once the rush here is over.'

'Another time?' he suggested.

'Thank you, I should like that.' She watched him as he went out of the room. Really too good-looking to be true, she thought, yet he seemed a pleasant person too. She turned her attention to other guests until she could join her mother and Aunt Catherine in their private room for dinner.

'Quite a good day, I think,' her mother observed, kicking off her shoes with a sigh of relief. 'I'd really like a long, hot bath at the moment,' she said, 'more than dinner.'

'Not me,' declared Gabrielle. 'I'm absolutely starved.'

The next day, Whit Monday, was equally busy. A brilliant morning was followed in the afternoon by squally showers, so that more people stayed in the hotel and there were more afternoon teas to be served. One or two guests took their departure and Howard Nelmes moved into a vacant room. Gabrielle could not take time off, and joined her parents and Catherine for dinner, tired out.

'Will Jim be all right in the bar with Tony?' Mrs. Knight asked her husband.

'Tony will look after things and Jim can do the fetching and carrying. Jim likes to be there in the bar.'

'That young Mrs. Moss was very good in the dining-room,' commented Aunt Catherine. Mrs. Moss came from the Village, which was an unending source of casual labour for the Tudor Rose, since most of the wives there were anxious to earn some money. They were spruced up, put into black dresses and frivolous white aprons, and took various kinds of left-overs home with them.

'Well, let her know we can use her during the summer, Catherine. By the way, Professor Haymer has booked in with his family for the whole of July. We badly need an annex here, Bill.'

'Or Medlicott House,' said her husband.

'Indeed, yes,' sighed Mrs. Knight.

'That reminds me,' said Gabrielle, 'this evening, Miss Medlicott is having dinner with Doctor Huwlett and his mother at their house.'

'No!' cried her mother, dismayed.

'Yes, I'm afraid so. I heard them arranging it. He had had lunch at Medlicott House when I went there the other afternoon.'

'He's getting his claws into that poor woman,' said Catherine. 'Why don't you both go along and see her, Pamela and Bill, and make her an outright offer?'

'We don't even know yet that she wants to sell the place.'

'Go and find out. You'll get nowhere by politely waiting. That Huwlett isn't politely waiting, you may be sure.'

'She didn't say anything to you, Gabrielle, that showed you what she was thinking?'

'I didn't have a chance to talk to her, because she was off to see her solicitor.'

'Well, do go and see her, darling, as soon as you have some leisure.'

As soon as Gabrielle was at leisure, however, it was not to see Miss Medlicott that she went. She found herself, instead, riding with Howard Nelmes, she on Chestnut, he on Robin Adair, hardly knowing how it had come about. The merest suggestion that he might get a mount from Colonel Reid-Browne had resulted in this. Not a man to waste time, Gabrielle thought.

They were riding up through the woods towards the old quarry, and Gabrielle was reminded of coming up here before to encounter the Land-Rover coasting carefully down. She pictured Ivor Huwlett performing an operation on an old kitchen table; she saw him again working on a badly injured man in the mud of a field on a dark, wet night; she remembered him in a procession of farm houses or cottages, doing more, surely, than was expected of a G.P., assuming the sort of responsibility for them that one might expect of a father confessor – which, in a way, he was.

'You're very thoughtful,' commented her companion.

Gabrielle turned a smiling face towards him and banished thoughts of Ivor Huwlett. They came out to the uplands and the wide-ranging views and the wind that always blew up there in varying degrees: sometimes not much more than a zephyr and sometimes a howling gale. Today it was pleasantly fresh and they rode higher and higher as the view grew wider and wider. They came to the old quarry, and there were the children playing around among some boulders with pieces of old rusty machinery, or running in and out of the broken walls of buildings that had fallen down long ago.

They were turned into statues by the arrival of the two riders. Gabrielle saw that there were four of them today, the two she had seen previously, a younger girl and an older boy.

'Hallo,' she said pleasantly, but only the boy, who had an appealing and impudent face, answered her: 'Hallo.'

'Are you the boy who had an appendicitis operation?' she asked him.

'Yes, miss.' Clear and confident.

'Better now?'

'Yes, miss.'

'When are you going back to school?'

There was a silence. Then he said:

'We don't go to school.'

Like a jack-in-the-box, the woman appeared at the door of the cottage, suspicion written all over her.

'Good afternoon,' said Gabrielle.

There was another child, perhaps two years old, hanging to her skirt, and Gabrielle saw that the woman was pregnant again.

'What do you want?' demanded the woman. 'Pokin' and pryin' up 'ere. What you askin' them questions for?'

'No reason,' said Gabrielle. 'I'm glad your boy is better now.' She turned her horse. 'We'd better go on,' she said to

Howard, and when they were out of earshot of the woman, she said: 'She has a horror of authority. If the authorities knew those children didn't go to school, there would be an outcry. If they knew they were there at all, there would be an outcry. She must live a life of perpetual anxiety. She knows that if they had to leave that awful place, the family would be broken up.'

'The children look happy enough,' he commented.

'But they're not being educated.' She shook off the subject. 'Want to go up further?' she asked. 'It's not so rough higher up.'

They had a satisfying canter at the top, and they dismounted for a while, where Howard tethered their mounts to a stunted hawthorn lying horizontally away from the wind, and Gabrielle identified for him the points of interest in that wide-ranging view. It was there at the top that he kissed her; and it was not an intrusive kiss or a demanding kiss, but quite natural so that Gabrielle could respond to it as naturally. They linked hands as they strolled about on the summit and their mounts cropped the sweet mountain grass; and when they rode back to leave the horses on the way to the Tudor Rose, a basis of admiring friendship had been established between them.

'Can we do it again?' he asked as they walked into the hotel.

'We're still pretty full. Lots of people take a week at Whitsun. But I'll see what I can do,' she promised him.

She had not forgotten her mother's request that she should go and see Miss Medlicott, and when she had some free time, it was to Medlicott House she turned and not Howard Nelmes. She drove there, wondering if once more the doctor's car would be on the drive. There was a car there, but it was not Ivor Huwlett's.

She was admitted by Susan, who always had a pleasant

smile for her, and was conducted to the drawing-room.

Miss Medlicott was not alone. Standing beside her, looking about him at the drawing-room with an obvious satisfaction, was an amazing figure of a man. He was middle-aged and enormous. His bushy hair had once been red but was now liberally sprinkled with pepper and salt. His voice was booming and echoing in the room, and Gabrielle thought she saw Miss Medlicott flinch; and he waved an unlit cigar between his fingers as his gesticulations accompanied his words.

He broke off as Gabrielle entered, regarding her with obvious pleasure.

'Ah, Gabrielle,' said Miss Medlicott in a faint voice, 'how very pleased I am to see you. This is Mr. Buss. Mr. Buss, Miss Knight.'

Mr. Buss held out an immense paw in which Gabrielle's slim hand was immediately lost.

'Mr. Buss,' Miss Medlicott explained in a voice which was almost expiring, 'is a builder. He has been looking at the house – er – assessing its possibilities.'

'That's right,' agreed Mr. Buss expansively. 'Just a preliminary investigation, as you might say. I take it, Miss Ivy, there's no objection to speaking in front of this little lady?' Miss Medlicott shook her head. 'Well, there's no doubt about it, when they built this place, they built it properly. None of your jerry-building here. I wouldn't be ashamed of it myself, and I can tell you that Joseph Buss's standards are as good as anybody's and better than most. Not that there aren't a few shortcomings, in the way of bathrooms and, let's say, a few other necessities.'

It seemed to Gabrielle that there was nothing that would stop his flow of speech unless somebody interrupted him.

'Miss Medlicott, do sit down,' she said. 'You look tired. I hope *you* haven't been trailing round the house assessing its

72

possibilities.'

Mr. Buss looked down from his great height, over his great girth, to the slim and small Miss Medlicott.

'Well now, you've overdone it,' he said sympathetically.

'You shouldn't have let her,' said Gabrielle mildly.

'Well now, I'd never dream of telling Miss Ivy what she could do or couldn't do,' he said. 'You sit down and take a breather,' he advised her. He turned back to Gabrielle. 'When I was a lad, I used to come and help in the stables here, every Saturday. It wasn't for money, lord bless you, they paid you next to nothing in those days; but because I loved the horses. Now Miss Ivy, she was a bit too young to boss me, but her sisters Miss Mabel and Miss Etty, they'd order me about as if they owned me, body and soul.'

At the moment, Miss Medlicott looked as if she were terrified of speaking to him at all.

'Loved horses all my life, I have,' he said. 'But I'd like to see the horse that'd carry me now.'

'Gabrielle, you'd like some tea. Mr. Buss, will you have some tea with us?'

He considered the problem for a moment, then agreed that a cup of tea would be very welcome.

'Perhaps you'd like to sit down,' suggested his hostess.

He looked about him – for a chair, Gabrielle suspected, that would take his weight – and selected a substantial armchair.

'Now,' he said, 'I'm going to think about your little problem, Miss Ivy. I've got the layout up here,' tapping his forehead, 'and I've got the alternative possibilities, or functions, as you might say. And I don't see why either of them shouldn't work very well; but of course, you can't have both. That's a fact. The one thing I do agree with you about is that you don't want a damn great place like this to yourself. You

73

might feel lost or lonely in it, but that's not the point. The point is that no one person should have all this amount of space, or' (waving his hand at the window) 'monopolize all of this lovely park, when lots of other people could enjoy it too.'

'You think that very selfish, Mr. Buss?'

'I do indeed, Miss Ivy. Not that I'd call *you* selfish, you understand. You've been brought up in a different way from me. But you could have a nice flat here, all the space you'd want, and still adopt one of those schemes of yours.' He looked at her as if she were a small pet he owned and was rather fond of. 'It would give me pleasure to fix up a flat for you – plenty of space – I know you're used to space . . .'

Susan rescued them by bringing in tea. Gabrielle thought that if Miss Medlicott had been enduring this for long, it was small wonder she looked tired and her voice had almost gone.

The sight of the tea tray silenced Mr. Buss. The thinness of the diminutive sandwiches, the fragility of the small cups, seemed to cause him some surprise. He took his cup warily – it looked ridiculous in that huge hand, a pint mug would have suited it better – but said almost at once: 'That's a nice piece of old Spode, that is,' in an appreciative voice. Gabrielle thought she would cut off the flow of his booming voice, and began to talk quietly to Miss Medlicott: of usual things like the weather and garden, of the busyness of the hotel over the Whitsun holiday. But the voice broke in again:

'Ah,' it said jovially. 'Now I've got you. Miss Knight. From the Tudor Rose?'

Gabrielle nodded.

'Many's the comfortable evening I've had in your dad's hotel. Now there's a nice place for you, they've made a real good job of that. You're the little girl that went off to work abroad, then, young Gabrielle? Well, you ask your mother and dad about Joe Buss. I've carried out many a job for them in my time.' A thought struck him. He said: 'I think I see daylight now, Miss Ivy. It wouldn't be Bill and Pamela Knight, would it . . .'

'Mr. Buss,' he was interrupted by Miss Medlicott, and stopped speaking at once. 'Please, I must ask you to regard what I have told you as a confidence.'

At last he went. He rose from his chair to his surprisingly great height, and crossed with heavy footsteps to Miss Medlicott's side.

'Now don't get up,' he said, restraining her with a hand on her shoulder although she had no intention of moving. She withdrew from the touch of that hand, which seemed as if it might push her through her chair. 'I'm going to keep in touch, Miss Ivy, and let you know what I come up with.' He nodded a dignified head at Gabrielle and went away. Miss Medlicott sighed her relief. Even Gabrielle, who found him fascinating, was relieved at the silence that followed his departure. They had a quiet cup of tea together.

'Did you ask him to come, Miss Medlicott?'

'No. I was asked if I would allow him to come.'

'It's rather like inviting Niagara into your drawing room.'

'He is said to be a very good builder, and clever, something of an artist. It's hard to believe.'

Who wanted him to come? wondered Gabrielle. He had mentioned her parents, but surely they would have told her about him. Could it be Ivor Huwlett, advancing his plans step by carefully planned step? What had happened at that dinner party at the Huwlett house on Monday evening?

As if conjured up by her thoughts of him, Ivor appeared at the door, shown in by Susan. Gabrielle thought that Miss Medlicott hardly suffered from a lack of company today.

'A quick moment only,' he said to Miss Medlicott, 'to bring you the report you said you would like to read.' He saw Gabrielle then. 'Ah, Gabrielle! I expected *you* to be snowed under by importunate guests.'

'Well, it's been rather hectic,' she said mildly.

'Tea, Dr. Huwlett?'

'No, thank you. If you'll forgive me, I haven't time to stay. I just wanted to know if Joe Buss had been along to see you yet.'

'Indeed, he has. He was here for nearly two hours.'

'Miss Medlicott was quite exhausted,' Gabrielle reproved him. Ivor laughed.

'Yes, he can be a bit overpowering,' he agreed, but apparently was not at all regretful that his hostess was overtired. He put the report down on the tea table. 'You will find that interesting,' he said. 'I shall look forward to discussing it with you.' As if, thought Gabrielle with an unusual touch of resentment, he was giving her her homework to do. 'And to hearing what conclusions Joe Buss comes to. Now please excuse me. Good-bye, Miss Medlicott, Gabrielle.'

And he was gone too. Miss Medlicott smiled as the door closed behind him.

'Men,' she said, out of her vast ignorance about them. 'What impulsive creatures they are! I must admit I have a great admiration for Dr. Huwlett.'

'*I* think he's disgustingly bossy,' said Gabrielle; and before her hostess could comment on that, added: 'So it was Ivor Huwlett who sent the Buss man along?'

'Yes. I see that I shall have the greatest difficulty in resisting any pressures they put upon me. *You* must come to my rescue, Gabrielle.'

'I shall be delighted,' Gabrielle promised her.

At the Tudor Rose, everybody was charmed with Howard

Nelmes. Most people, influenced by his exceptional good looks, thought he must be in show business. Gabrielle told him this when they were once more riding together. They had enjoyed a good gallop over the hills and now were jogging slowly along, side by side.

'On the contrary,' he said. 'I am a hard-headed man of business. I've just completed a world tour, visiting our branches, agents and contacts in many countries.'

'That accounts for the deep tan,' said Gabrielle.

'Yes: although you'd be surprised how much of the time was spent in aeroplanes and at airports. It's my job to go round seeing that everybody is doing what he's supposed to do; and finding new agents and making new contacts.'

Although she had known him only a few days, Gabrielle thought he would be good at that. He seemed to have an unflappable personality, he was pleasant to everybody and he was good at listening.

'I have a fair amount of leave due to me,' he said, 'which, because I'm really quite absorbed in my work, I haven't bothered to use up. I have an idea I'm now going to make inroads into it, by coming to the Tudor Rose as often as you will put up with me.'

'I don't find it hard to put up with you,' she told him smilingly.

'And it must be fairly obvious to you, Gay, that I find it hard to keep away from you.'

'That's all right with me,' she said, and he stretched a hand out to her and she put hers into it – until their horses moved apart and the warm clasp was broken.

They came down from the hilltops to a narrow lane, still jogging peacefully side by side, and rounded a bend to find themselves facing a Land-Rover. The Land-Rover immediately stopped, the driver not wanting to scare the horses. Gabrielle went in front of Howard to pass by.

'Thank you,' she said to the driver.

'Business is still very hectic, I see,' he said to her.

'Even *I* have time off sometimes,' she said, mocking him. 'Howard, this is Dr. Huwlett. Ivor, Howard Nelmes.'

The men greeted each other, both of them taking stock.

'I'm on my way to see Mrs. Barnes,' Ivor told Gabrielle.

It took her a moment to remember Mrs. Barnes.

'Do give her my kind regards,' she said.

'She's had a fall. The postman brought me the message – he takes her bread and milk, you remember. I don't know what I shall find there.'

'Can I help?'

'I'll let you know. If she's broken anything, I'll have her down in the Cottage Hospital. She won't like it, but there ...' He nodded at Howard, looked thoughtfully at Gabrielle, and the moment the horses had passed, started his engine and was off up the narrow road.

'A friend of yours?' Howard asked her watchfully.

'Mrs. Barnes? No, I hardly know her.'

'I meant the doctor.'

'Oh, him! No, I'd hardly say a *friend*.'

'Something more than a friend?'

She suddenly saw where his questions led. She had been thinking of the doctor. Now she banished him.

'Something more like an enemy,' she said crisply.

Howard was reassured. He wanted to ask if there was anybody else he had to take into consideration, but thought that might be left until his next visit. But Gabrielle occupied most of his thoughts on that first visit to the Tudor Rose.

When she drove into the Town on an errand for her mother, Howard accompanied her. When he walked through the lounge hall, he stopped at her reception counter for a

78

chat with her. He lured her into the comfortable bar for a drink before dinner; and late at night he kept a lookout for her, so that they might walk along the road by the lake. A couple of times he took a boat out on the lake, to fish. Gabrielle, seeing him from one of the upper windows, watched him thoughtfully, a little wistfully.

His week came to an end all too quickly.

'I'm sorry to go,' he said to Gabrielle, paying his bill.

'We're sorry to see you go,' she said, remembering the loving kiss with which they had parted last night.

'I'll be back, that's for sure.'

'Let me know in time to fix you up, we get so busy later.'

'I can always fall back on Mrs. Thomas.'

'We'll try to find you a corner, anyway.'

'Yes, keep one for me,' he said. 'A warm corner.'

She went out to wave him good-bye, and stood dreamily watching the spot where his car had disappeared from sight. She had felt amazingly comfortable and at her ease with him. She would indeed keep a warm corner in her thoughts for him and looked forward to the time when he would come again.

From Whitsun on, the tempo of work in the hotel increased. It was so deservedly popular that they had to turn many people away, and their thoughts turned with increasing longing to Medlicott House standing so empty on such a beautiful site. Gabrielle went on with her office work and reception duties, arranged flowers, advised guests about their tours, kept an eye on the lounge hall from her desk, so that ash trays were promptly emptied, tea trays removed, odd litter left by visitors promptly disposed of. Occasionally there were guests from abroad, but many of these spoke such excellent English that Gabrielle was afraid her languages would never be used.

Extra staff was recruited from the Village. The hotel van shuttled them to and fro on a complicated shift system that suited their families' needs and also those of the hotel. Gabrielle had little time for calling on Miss Medlicott and had not seen the doctor for some time.

Until, early one afternoon, Miss Medlicott telephoned her, the first time she had done so.

'Gabrielle, I expect you are very busy?'

'We have been, Miss Medlicott. I'm sorry I haven't been to see you lately.'

'I *was* wondering, Gabrielle, if you could come this afternoon. I realize, of course, that it may be out of the question. Do say so if it's impossible. But I feel the need of support. That man is here.'

Gabrielle thought 'that man' could mean only one person.

'Mr. Buss?'

'Yes. I admit he alarms me. It's like having a huge clumsy dog in the house who might bowl one over at any moment.'

'I'll do my best to come right over,' said Gabrielle.

There seemed to be a dearth of people who could take over the reception counter. Her parents were nowhere to be seen, and Mary was having an afternoon off. She decided to rouse Catherine, who liked a nap after lunch. Catherine, hearing the purpose of Gabrielle's visit, agreed at once to look after reception, and Gabrielle drove to Medlicott House.

Mr. Buss, in a pepper-and-salt tweed suit, which could hardly have been more unsuitable on this summer afternoon, looked rather like the huge shaggy dog Miss Medlicott had likened him to. Gabrielle heard his powerful voice before she reached the drawing-room, where they both turned and greeted her with pleasure.

'I've been telling Miss Ivy that she wants to get rid of some of her trees,' he said. 'Trees and shrubs are all very well, and some of the specimen trees here are superb, they should have a preservation order. But enough is enough. I've been telling her, Miss Gabrielle, that she could have a new vista down to the lake over in that direction,' he waved an arm, 'if she got rid of some of the vegetation that's nothing special at all.' He walked to the long french window. 'Come and see what I mean,' he invited Gabrielle.

Gabrielle followed him and stepped out on to the terrace. Miss Medlicott hesitated, then went too.

'There's already this beautiful vista down to the lake,' Gabrielle reminded him, looking straight ahead.

'Now you look round here. Two massive rhododendrons would have to go, but there are so many two wouldn't be missed; and behind you've only got silver birch, dogwood and hazel. Can you see the lake there?'

Gabrielle perched herself on the base of a column that supported nothing but climbing roses, and stretched her neck.

'Yes, I see what you mean,' she admitted.

'Do you see, Miss Medlicott?' he asked, and she shook her head.

'No, you're so much taller than I, but I remember when I was a girl, we could see the lake from here.'

Without more ado, Mr. Joseph Buss put a huge hand on each side of Miss Medlicott's waist and lifted her as easily as if she had been a doll, so that she could see what he had in mind. Gabrielle looked at him in astonishment. After several seconds he put her down again as carefully as if she were a piece of fragile china. Gabrielle saw that she had blushed a dark red, taken completely by surprise. Probably no man had touched her for years. The painful blush died away only slowly, and left her so white that Gabrielle wondered if she was going to faint. She stepped into the breach.

'I do think you have a point, Mr. Buss,' she said, smiling up at him, distracting his attention from his hostess. She was aware of Miss Medlicott straightening her suit, trying to regain her composure. 'It would make a lovely walk down to the lake. The point is whether the work and expense would be justified.'

'From the aesthetic point of view alone it would be justified.' He put an arm carefully about Miss Medlicott's narrow shoulders. 'Now don't you agree with me, Miss Ivy?'

'I really don't know,' she said. She was agitated. 'Gabrielle, Mr. Buss will have my own house down about my ears and my grounds lying in destruction.'

'No, no,' he protested, and it was a roar that shook both women. 'I'm no vandal, Miss Ivy. I'm no Philistine. Whatever use you put your house to, it would be an improvement.'

She moved away from the heavy arm round her shoulders.

'Sometimes,' she said tiredly, 'I think I'll just sell it.'

'You could do that, of course,' judicially, 'if you could bear to leave it. But *I* don't think you could leave it, Miss Ivy. What you'd better do – and think about this, my dear girl, because it's a good idea – is let me make a house for you out of that coachhouse. You could have a little beauty there. I'm going to think about that.'

'Mr. Buss.' Miss Medlicott's voice was growing desperate. 'Would you excuse me now? I want to have a little conversation with Gabrielle.'

'Of course, of course.' He took her hand and shook it heartily. Gabrielle felt really sorry for her. 'I'll come again, with plans for that coachhouse. I'm really getting enthusiastic about this project.' He did not return to the house, but went away round the side of it to his waiting car.

'What a dreadful man,' said Miss Medlicott faintly.

'He obviously thinks the world of you.'

'Well, I wish he didn't. If he gets really enthusiastic about this project, as he calls it, I don't know how I shall stand it. I don't think I'd ever be able to say No to him, or that he'd take any notice if I did.'

'I'm sure he would. Of course, he might fight every inch of the way.'

'You see? How exhausting it would be. Already, I feel quite battered, and the thought of future battles daunts me.' She turned to go back into the drawing-room. 'Already, I feel that nothing is going to stop him making that new vista down to the lake.'

'Dear Miss Medlicott, he can't do anything without your say-so; and if you don't like to tackle him yourself, I'll do it for you.'

'No, no, I mustn't rely on others. I must be able to stand on my own feet.'

Suddenly, Gabrielle realized that this was something she had never had to do. From her parents and from Miss Medlicott herself, Gabrielle had gathered a picture of what her life had been like in this great house: private, sheltered, shutting out the world. And the other two sisters had been much older. It was they who had taken the decisions, who had taken Ivy into their own uneventful orbit and their already-planned existence. They had drawn in upon themselves, been enough for each other. No wonder Mr. Buss terrified Miss Medlicott.

When Gabrielle left, she found herself very angry with Ivor Huwlett, who had let this ogre of a man loose upon such a defenceless woman. And of course, he had done so to further his own ends. It went without saying that he would only introduce into Medlicott House a builder who would have sympathy with his own ambitions and who would advise Miss Medlicott to turn her house into old people's flats. And poor Miss Medlicott would be putty in the hands of two such determined men, the more so as her previous experience of men seemed to be nil.

Gabrielle hesitated when she came to the end of the drive, then, instead of turning in the direction of the Tudor Rose, she drove in the opposite direction towards the doctor's house; with the vague intention, if she happened to see him, of telling him what she thought of him and of asking him to call off his alarming watchdog.

The gravel in front of the doctor's house, however, was free of cars. Gabrielle could not remember which were his afternoons at the distant hospital. He might even be at the local small cottage hospital, or simply on an afternoon round of calls. It was most unlikely that she would see him, yet she found herself driving on into the grey shabbiness of the Village and to its further end, before she turned to go home.

The contrast between this place, its dark stone shut in by dark hills, and the valley where it widened out into the lake, was very marked: the hills suddenly greener, room for the trees to grow. Nature became expansive, more beautiful. The lake itself had small wavelets running across it today and the clouds over the opposite hills were scudding swiftly. Gabrielle was absorbed in her surroundings and had forgotten the doctor, when suddenly she came upon his car parked in a lay-by at the side of the road. She braked swiftly, and he looked up from a book in which he was writing, to see the cause of the sudden braking.

'I wanted to talk to you,' she said to him, and backed her car, and brought it to his side of the road in the lay-by.

'Well, here I am. Can you give me a moment?'

She got out of her car and went to the side of his. He

finished what he was writing, put the cap back on his pen and smiled at her.

'At your service. I'll get out and have a breather.'

He stood beside her in the heavy shade of trees that overhung from both sides, meeting overhead.

'It was you,' she said, 'who sent that ogre of a man to Miss Medlicott.'

'You mean Joe Buss, I presume?'

'I mean Mr. Buss.'

'You make it sound like an accusation.'

'That's what it is. He frightens her.'

'Nonsense,' Ivor laughed. 'He's a harmless old bear.'

'Not to her. She gets most agitated and finds him completely overpowering. Why, she rings me up to go and rescue her.'

'My dear Gabrielle, she's not a nun in an enclosed order.'

'That's just what she is, in effect. She's not used to men at all – oh, maybe the vicar and the solicitor and the doctor . . .'

'Thanks,' said Ivor.

'Oh, I didn't mean you, I was thinking of old Dr. Pasture. But she isn't used to men, and you send one who is just too big and booming in every way.'

'He'll do her good,' said Ivor.

'Not at all. He puts an arm around her shoulders and she shrinks away. He lifts her up to look over some bushes and she almost passes out. She thinks he'll override her in everything, and that she won't be able to say No to him.'

'Joe won't override her. He'll bring his ideas to me. And Miss Medlicott has the final word about everything. Nobody's going to hustle her into anything.'

'That's just what you are doing,' said Gabrielle hotly, 'and losing no time about it either.'

'Ah,' said Ivor, as if everything was clear to him.

'What do you mean – Ah?'

'I mean that now we can come to the nub of the matter.'

'Can't you speak in plain English?'

'I thought I was. Very well, in plain English, your concern is not for Miss Medlicott but for your own plans for Medlicott House.'

'That's not true! I was thinking of her!'

'Partly, perhaps, but most of this anger is because you think you may not get that house for a hotel.'

So it was out in the open between them now.

'And your concern to get Joe Buss in so quickly is because you're frightened you may not get it for your old people.'

'Which, in my opinion, is a worthier cause.'

'In *your* opinion,' she said scathingly, 'the only worthy people are sick or old ones. You seem to think nobody else has any sympathy for them. Everybody has . . .'

'Sympathy,' he interrupted her, 'that stops short of doing anything for them.'

'Not at all. But not everybody works for the sick or old. There are other people who need relaxation, and who *deserve* it too. People we look after in hotels, who work just as hard as you do all the year round, and come to us for a holiday. It's a different kind of service, but it is a service – not that I expect you to admit it.'

'It may be. Go on giving service – you can do it at the Tudor Rose. I've got nowhere to gather up my lonely old people stuck in remote places; but if I can get Medlicott House for them, I will.'

'You seem to be working very hard at it.'

'Unfortunately I'm not, because I don't have the time for it. I assure you I shall work on her as much as I can . . .'

'As you tried to work on me,' cried Gabrielle.

'Oh, I haven't given up on you yet,' he said easily.

'You – are – maddening! I'd like to shake some sense into you.'

He smiled at her.

'If it will let off steam, you're welcome,' he said.

She shrugged her shoulders, sighing with frustration. He reached out his arms to her and, for a moment, she thought he was going to give her the shaking she had wanted to give him. Instead, he wrapped his arms around her and kissed her closely, completely and passionately; and she was so surprised that she offered no resistance whatever. When he gently released her, she stood in a daze, unable immediately to remember what they had been talking about.

'Whatever did you do that for?' she asked.

Ivor was watching her with bright, dark eyes.

'It seems to have taken the wind out of your sails, at any rate,' he observed.

It had. She was almost struck dumb. He laughed.

'I did it,' he said, 'because you were angry. I can't resist angry women. Their eyes flash fire and their cheeks colour up and they lose their inhibitions – and I feel like kissing them. So be warned.'

'That isn't a joke that appeals to me,' she said coldly. She turned away to her car, remembering that she hadn't stopped to talk personalities with him. 'Well, are you going to call off your watchdog?' she asked.

'No.'

'Not even when you know he upsets Miss Medlicott.'

'He won't go on upsetting her. I'll have a little talk with him. Not that I'd want him to change his charming and expansive character. And I'll explain him to poor little Miss Medlicott too.'

'*Rich* little Miss Medlicott. *You* wouldn't be interested in her otherwise.'

'Now that, I think, is the nastiest thing you've said to me

to date,' he said. 'I think it needs an apology.'

'Well, it isn't getting one,' said Gabrielle, and closed her car door, started the engine, and drove away from him. He watched her go, then drove off in the opposite direction.

Almost at once, Gabrielle had qualms of conscience. It was so patently obvious that it was not rich people that interested him as a rule. He felt almost too much obligation to his poor patients: and it was for lonely people, poor and otherwise, that he wanted Medlicott House. It *had* been a nasty thing to say. She should have apologized. She felt rather wretched, rather displeased with herself, as she drove into the courtyard of the Tudor Rose.

CHAPTER FIVE

GABRIELLE'S hand reached out towards the telephone, rested on the receiver for some time while she considered, and then withdrew. She turned to her accounts and began to make up bills; but she was still undecided, and stopped her work to think again.

Once again, she reached for the telephone and this time lifted the receiver and dialled a number.

A woman's voice answered, and she asked to speak to Dr. Huwlett.

'Who is calling, please?'

'Miss Knight.'

'Well, I'm sorry, Miss Knight, the doctor is very busy at the moment. Will you leave a message, or will you call again? . . . Oh, just a moment, please, the doctor says he will speak to you.'

There was an appreciable pause. Gabrielle felt that she would have rung off if she had not already given her name. Then she heard Ivor's voice.

'Sorry to keep you waiting. I'm in surgery. I was changing a dressing.'

'I'm sorry to interrupt you, especially as it's nothing important.' Conscious that she was wasting time that *was* important, she hurried on: 'You felt that an apology was due from me, Ivor. I think so, too, and so I'm offering you one.'

'Why, thank you.' He sounded surprised. 'That's very handsome.' There was a brief pause and then he said, and there was a hint of a smile in his voice: 'Ah shore do appreciate that, ma'am.' And the click of the receiver told her that he had rung off.

She was left feeling defrauded. What had she expected? A long post-mortem on the dissension between them? More credit for sinking her pride and apologizing? But that was absurd. There he was, engrossed in his work, changing the dressing on what might be a bad wound, even a gruesome one, and a stupid woman interrupts him with a trivial apology for rudeness! Still, it was now off her mind. She should be feeling relieved. And she wondered why she was not, why the short interchange had been so inconclusive, left her feeling unsettled.

Mary had just arrived at the reception counter to take Gabrielle's place while she went to lunch, when Ivor telephoned her.

'Ah, Gabrielle,' he said. 'I was sorry to be so brief this morning. I was in the middle of something I couldn't leave. I simply want to thank you for your gesture and to tell you that all is forgiven and forgotten.'

She made a sound that might have been laughter or might have been a snort of derision. She said:

'I'm only just learning when to take you seriously and when you are being flippant.'

'Flippant? I'm the most serious soul in the world. Shall we cement the end of our differences by riding together on Sunday morning?'

'Oh, I'm sorry, I can't do that. I've already promised to go riding with somebody else.'

'Ah.' She was growing accustomed to those deliberating 'Ahs' of his. 'Pity. Would it be with this Howard friend of yours?'

'It would,' said Gabrielle.

'Never mind. It's quite a long time since I had a round of golf. It will be equally good exercise.'

'Good golfing,' she wished him, wondering if exercise was

his only reason for suggesting to ride with her.

'Good riding, Gabrielle. And good-bye.'

Even after this call, she was not entirely content. She would have liked to ride with him, but she did not think that either of the men would want to make a threesome.

So she rode with Howard on Sunday morning and enjoyed herself so much, was so light-hearted with him and so much at ease, that she did not give the doctor a thought. He, on the other hand, did not particularly enjoy his golf. He was out of practice and played badly and was glad to get home again, to change his clothes before going to lunch with Miss Medlicott. His mother, knowing he was going out, had also gone to lunch with friends. He switched on the telephone answering service to find out if anything was urgent, and decided he could go out with a clear conscience. He set the answering service again, checked that his bag was in the car, and went out to lunch.

He and Miss Medlicott spent a pleasant half-hour with pre-lunch drinks on the terrace, while Ivor absent-mindedly demolished the appetizing tit-bits the cook provided, then went in to the kind of lunch he did not eat every day; and then lazed on the terrace again afterwards with their coffee.

Ivor thought it truly was an idyllic place. The sun shone (so that Miss Medlicott sat under the shade of a huge blue umbrella), the swans sailed slowly and regally on the placid surface of the lake; and over the hills opposite, puffs of white cloud were almost motionless. They lingered over coffee and then took a walk through the grounds and along the edge of the lake, talking, talking. Most of the time they talked of Miss Medlicott's future and the future of her house. It was a topic that absorbed them both.

She was asking him to stay to tea, when Susan came hurrying down the terrace steps saying the doctor was needed on the telephone.

'Ivor,' said his mother, 'two urgent things. I just got in, and one was already on the answering service. A boy called Ted Wade was knocked off his bike by a car – that group of small houses where you turn off the lake road for the town; and Granny Truscott has fallen downstairs in her house in the Village, and the family is scared to move her. Miles away from each other! So I rang Pasture, and he *would* be away for the day.'

'Ring Nurse Harper. She'll go to the boy. If it's necessary, she'll get an ambulance. She'll know whether Cottage Hospital or the other. I'll get there as soon as I can. About Mrs. Truscott, she is still alive, I suppose?'

'She was when they rang, but they don't know how badly she is hurt.'

'O.K. I'll go at once.'

Miss Medlicott had reached him by now.

'Yes, go at once,' she said. 'Don't delay.' And he went quickly out to his car.

Sunday traffic! he thought. How some of it dawdled! He knew the road so well that he knew exactly where it was safe to overtake and where it was not. Other drivers cursed him. 'Look at that fool,' they said, 'Trying to break his neck.' But that was the last thing Ivor wanted to do. On the contrary, he was trying to save other people's.

It was hours before he was free to go home. Granny Truscott was in the Cottage Hospital surrounded by her loving family. She was the sort of independent old lady who *would* do things for herself. Good thing *she* didn't live alone, thought Ivor, or she would be at the bottom of the stairs yet. The boy, Ted Wade, with a broken leg, was at the big hospital. Ivor had had a few words with the indispensable Nurse Harper, and they stood together on the pavement in the easy companionship of long years of harmonious working together.

'Well, what now?' asked Ivor.

She shrugged her shoulders.

'Too late for church.'

'I feel like a drink,' he said. 'Let's go and have one.'

'Would they be open?'

'Just about.'

'The only decent place is the Tudor Rose, and you don't go there.'

'Come back with me, then, Pat.'

Mrs. Huwlett welcomed them, told them to go and sit on the verandah, and took drinks out for them. It was a pleasant, rambling garden, not too well kept. No Medlicott, thought Ivor, contentedly sunk into his old basket chair, but not bad either. He realized that he had a warm and satisfied feeling, and it did not take him long to trace it back to its source. He had been caught up suddenly by his work and it had injected new life into him.

He caught Pat Harper's eye and smiled at her. Over her drink, she smiled back at him.

'D'you know,' she said, 'I was having such a boring afternoon until your mother phoned. All week, I look forward to putting my feet up at the weekend with a good book – or even a bad one – and then, come Sunday, I sometimes get so bored. And now I'm all smoothed out and virtuous.'

'Dear Pat, you're a mind-reader.'

'You feeling the same?'

'I can't say I was bored exactly. But something the same.'

She was contented, too, to be admitted into the circle of his friends. Yet not entirely content, because she always hoped for more. She stayed to supper with him after ringing up her parents. On condition, said Mrs. Huwlett, that they didn't talk shop. She really had enough of nurses and doctors. But none of them could really keep away from it.

Howard Nelmes was staying at the Tudor Rose again for a week, and during that week every moment of spare time that Gabrielle had was monopolized by him. They rode again, they walked on the hills, rowed on the lake, slipped out together after dinner to walk in the soft summer nights. All the Knights approved of him.

'They make such a beautiful couple,' said Catherine, watching them walk down to the small boathouse together. 'They're both so nice-looking and have such nice personalities.'

'Well, don't start matchmaking,' said Mrs. Knight. 'I've only just got Gay home, I don't want to lose her yet.'

It did seem, however, that Howard Nelmes had been swept off his feet by Gabrielle.

'My friends can't understand what's happened to me,' he told her. 'Though I expect some of them have their suspicions. I don't accept invitations for weekends because I intend to come here; and I rather resent having to pop over to Paris or Madrid or Lisbon, all places that used to have great attraction for me.'

'It's such a long way to drive here for a short weekend.'

'I shall have to get a helicopter,' he said. 'I had a plane once, but my fellow directors thought I was risking my neck too often, and now it's written into my contract: no flying my own plane.'

'I should think you'd find it dull coming here, after such an exciting existence.'

'Do you find it dull, after Zurich and all those other places?'

'Of course not, but I *love* it here.'

'Well, so do I love it.'

One afternoon that week, a fine, fresh summer afternoon,

they took Miss Medlicott for a drive. She did not drive herself – none of the sisters had – and did not like to take the chauffeur-gardener away from his garden to drive the car. So Gabrielle and Howard took her out, and back to tea at the Tudor Rose; and when they had driven her home again, she pressed them to stay for a drink, and they sat out on the terrace, where Ivor had sat the Sunday before, looking out over the same enchanting and peaceful view.

'After all your kindness to me, Gabrielle,' Miss Medlicott said, 'I hardly like to ask you to do me a favour again tomorrow.'

'Please do.'

'I have Mr. Buss coming at eleven in the morning, and really I don't feel quite like coping with him alone. Could you possibly come along at about that time? But not, of course, if you are too busy. He says he is anxious to tell me what *he* considers the best use for Medlicott House.'

Gabrielle thought she could not bear to miss that session; nor, as her parents' emissary, would they want her to. So she gladly promised to go along the following morning.

When they left, Howard said:

'Is she selling that beautiful place?'

'Yes, but hoping to reserve part of it for herself.'

'What is it going to be?'

'Nobody knows yet. My parents want it for a hotel. Can you imagine what a marvellous hotel it would make? But the local doctor wants it too, for flats for old people; but where the money would come from for such a scheme I can't think.'

'I suppose he could get grants for such a purpose.'

'But not for the entire sum. But then I'm quite prepared to believe he has already cooked up various schemes for getting money. So far, Miss Medlicott hasn't declared herself. I know that Dr. Huwlett has been working on her. So have I, for that matter. Perhaps tomorrow will see.'

She was rather silent on the drive back to the Tudor Rose. She was thinking of the pleasure Miss Medlicott had had from the afternoon's outing in the company of herself and Howard. And if Miss Medlicott, why not other people too? Why not Mrs. Barnes, up in that isolated hillside cottage? and others like her, who had not Miss Medlicott's other advantages. She had to admit that the doctor had a point, in wanting to give them a life that was more sociable and neighbours who might prove to be friends.

Next morning she left Howard to his own devices and was at Medlicott House soon after eleven. Mr. Buss was already there, identified by his booming voice before Gabrielle reached the drawing-room.

Miss Medlicott asked for sherry to be brought.

'Not for me, Miss Ivy,' said Mr. Buss. 'I'd much prefer a glass of beer, thank you.'

'Beer?' Miss Medlicott looked at Susan helplessly. 'I shouldn't think we have such a thing in the house, have we, Susan?'

'I'll inquire,' Susan said; and, having inquired, appeared with beer in a handsome tankard of a size that made Miss Medlicott blink.

'How very gratifying,' she said. 'I wonder who drinks it.' Gabrielle glanced at Mr. Buss and saw a twinkle in his eye and could not resist smiling at him. No doubt the gardener and his assistant had a weakness in that direction, if not Cook herself, or even Susan. Mr. Buss took a mighty swallow and Miss Medlicott watched warily, sipping delicately at her glass of sherry and quite unable to offer him a biscuit, which seemed so unsuitable and far too small.

'Well now,' said Mr. Buss. He had rolls of plans with him but did not open them. 'I've given the matter of this house a great deal of thought, Miss Ivy; and I know what conclusion

I've come to. What I want to know, before I say any more, is what feelings you have about it yourself.'

'I have had very mixed feelings from the beginning, Mr. Buss, which is why I am relying on outside, expert help. I do very much like the doctor's idea, I have a great deal of sympathy for his cause. I do feel, however, that the house would need a great deal of adaptation and might well lose its character; but perhaps that isn't the important thing. And then, you see, if the Knight family had its way and turned it into a hotel, it would undoubtedly give enormous pleasure to people that way. I really need advice, Mr. Buss. I would like to know what you think.'

Gabrielle thought it hardly necessary to ask him. He would do what his friend Ivor Huwlett wanted. If Miss Medlicott had mixed feelings, she was not alone. Gabrielle's were none too clear.

Mr. Buss kept them in suspense. Not intentionally. He finished his beer in a long gulp, set down his tankard and wiped his mouth with a spotless handkerchief.

'In my opinion,' he said, 'there's only one use to put this house to.' Here it comes, thought Gabrielle. 'It would make a first-class hotel, a five-star, if that's what one wanted.' And here comes the 'but' thought Gabrielle. 'And that, in my opinion, is what it ought to be,' he said. And stopped speaking.

Both the women stared at him. Both had expected him to take the other side.

Having thrown his bombshell and waited to see its effect, Mr. Buss began to speak again.

'I started out with the firm intention of doing what I could for Dr. Huwlett. And before I say another word, I'd like to say here what I think about Dr. Huwlett. The people here have more than they deserve in such a doctor – though one shouldn't say that since every patient deserves the best.

But he could go anywhere, do anything, of that I'm certain. But I've always said, London's loss is our gain. He doesn't stay here to make his fortune – far from it; nor to lead an idle life. He stays here to serve the people and I admire the service he gives.

'So, as I say, I started out to help him; and that meant persuading our little Miss Ivy here to turn her house into flats. But I can't advise her to do it. That's how it's turned out. I don't want to see this house chopped up in the way it would have to be chopped up. The plain fact is, it's not suitable. Just start with all these reception rooms. Are they to be cut up with partitions, with bathrooms and water closets put in? You wouldn't need reception rooms; even if you left the garden room for the common use of the residents. It would be a sheer waste, and it wouldn't make flats that were all that convenient.

'But now, as a hotel, it's got everything. Lounge hall, drawing-room, dining-room, small bar, TV room, and beautiful bedrooms. One must fit in bathrooms, of course, but there's plenty of space to play with. But the house retains its character completely. If I were you, Miss Ivy, I should sell it to the Knights, or whoever you choose, as a hotel.'

'But poor Dr. Huwlett,' said Miss Medlicott.

'It would cost a fortune to convert,' he said. 'It'll cost only a fraction of that for a hotel. And anyway, much better to start from scratch for the old people, and give them good new, labour-saving places.'

'They'd never get a site like this.' Gabrielle said it in spite of herself; knowing how overjoyed her parents would be if Miss Medlicott accepted Mr. Buss's verdict, and how furious Ivor would be.

'This isn't the only beautiful site in this part of the world; though I grant you these grounds take a lot of beating. Well, there it is, that's my opinion for what it's worth.'

'It's worth a great deal, Mr. Buss. I think you've been very honest; and I must admit that, deep down, I really do agree with you. So *much* reconstruction would have been needed; but all the same, I don't know how I shall face Dr. Huwlett with this news.'

'I'll do that for you, Miss Ivy.'

'Not at all.' She drew herself up to her full five-feet-two. 'I shouldn't dream of delegating my unpleasant tasks. I will speak to him myself.'

Mr. Buss looked at her with unconcealed admiration.

'Now about you,' he said affectionately. 'You don't want to live in a hotel. That coachhouse is going to make you a beautiful home with your own garden round it. You come with me, my dear girl, and I'll show you what I have in mind.' He extended a hand, took hers, put an enormous arm about her slender shoulders and led her towards the french windows.

'Will you come too, Gabrielle?'

'I really ought to be getting back,' Gabrielle pleaded.

'That's all right.' Mr. Buss nodded to her to be off. 'This just concerns Miss Ivy. I'll look after her.'

Miss Medlicott's glance seemed to accuse Gabrielle of deserting her in her hour of need; but Gabrielle had decided by now that Mr. Buss was what Ivor had declared him to be – a harmless old bear. It was even possible that something else Ivor had said might be right, that Mr. Buss would be good for her.

Ivor nagged at the back of her mind like a toothache lightly drugged, but she refused to pay attention to him. She drove speedily back to her home, went quickly through the lounge hall where some residents were having pre-lunch drinks, but Howard not among them, beckoned her mother from the dining-room, fetched Catherine from the kitchen, and said:

'Where's Dad?'

He was in the bar, but at Catherine's insistence, left it to Tony and joined the others in the private room.

'What's going on?' he asked.

Gabrielle told them, briefly and to the point.

'But don't take it as settled. Anything could happen. Ivor will try to persuade her. But at the moment she agrees with Mr. Buss, and if I were you, Dad, I'd get in touch with her . . .'

'Oh, Bill,' said Mrs. Knight, 'it can't be coming true at last, can it?' Her eyes were shining. Her husband put an arm around her.

'Don't count your chickens, love,' he said. 'Not yet.'

'Gabrielle, I've dreamed about this for years. It was only a sort of relaxation, just playing. . . . Because, after all, the sisters might have outlived us.'

'Not you,' interrupted her husband. 'You're still a youngster.'

She smiled at him affectionately. Gabrielle said:

'Can you really bear to leave the Tudor Rose?'

'But we wouldn't,' cried her mother. 'We'd have both.'

'*I* would run the Rose,' said Catherine. 'God knows I've served a long enough apprenticeship.'

Brother and sister looked at each other. Mr. Knight left his wife and went and put an arm round Catherine.

'You certainly have, lass,' he said. 'If you want to run the Rose, she's yours.'

'Provided you get Medlicott House,' said Gabrielle drily.

Her Aunt Catherine looked at her shrewdly.

'That's going to be a body blow for Ivor Huwlett,' she said. 'Thank goodness we've put one over on the Huwletts at last. I can't tell you what satisfaction that gives me.'

Gabrielle turned away. That nagging ache at the back of her mind became a sudden searing pain. It gave her no satisfaction at all to have scored over Dr. Huwlett.

From the moment she heard Gabrielle's news, Mrs. Knight went about like a woman transformed. She reminded herself constantly that something could go wrong, but radiated happiness. The effect of it was felt throughout the hotel. She beamed upon everybody, and hugged her moments of privacy to herself to dream of what she would do at Medlicott House.

She could not deny that the Tudor Rose had been a little goldmine. She and Bill and Catherine had given good service and good value for money, had always maintained their standards and had kept the kind of clientele they wanted. But the Tudor Rose had two drawbacks. It was not large enough and the building of an annex was not the ideal solution; and the road ran between the hotel and the lake, and became busier with each year of increasing traffic. Mrs. Knight thought of that splendid terrace and the steps widening out in a graceful curve to the lawn sweeping down to the water. And all the cars would be on the other side of the hotel, unheard, unseen; and a long drive cut the house off from the road.

'We must take the first steps,' she said to her husband and Gabrielle. 'I know these things take time. We don't know if her sisters' wills are proved yet. And then buying a place can be a long-drawn-out business. But that suits us, really, because we're embarked on quite a heavy season here. But how marvellous it would be, Bill, if we could open for next year.'

They tried to restrain her, but it was impossible. Her imagination had taken wings. Chandeliers, carpets, furniture. . . . Her husband groaned. 'Don't go living in Cloud-cuckoo Land,' he implored her, and said to Gabrielle: 'Your mother's only letting herself in for a stupendous disappointment if something goes amiss.'

Gabrielle could not share in this state of euphoria. She knew that she would have resented the doctor's success, but she could not bear his failure.

She knew that her parents called on Miss Medlicott and later lunched with her, and that those first steps had been taken; but she did not wish to be present. She wanted to speak to Miss Medlicott alone to find out how Ivor had taken the decision.

When she did go for morning sherry, on a gently drizzling summer day, she found a livelier and more alert Miss Medlicott. Gabrielle thought she was glad to have come to a decision and was now prepared to be interested in everything going on.

'So much is happening, Gabrielle. I realize how very quietly my sisters and I lived here. Of course I can't leave here until I have a house to live in, so Mr. Buss is making what he calls a "priority job" of turning the coachhouse into an ideal house for me. He advises an architect, but I hardly think it necessary as Mr. Buss seems to be a man of great experience. Would you like to see the plans?'

Gabrielle not only saw the plans but walked to the attractive coachhouse to see where the transformation would take place. As they walked back again to the house, she said:

'What about Dr. Huwlett, Miss Medlicott? How did he take your decision?'

'I'm afraid he was very disappointed. I was really very sorry about that, Gabrielle. I do admire him so much.'

'What did he say?'

'He didn't really say anything. He was very quiet. In fact, he was quiet for a long time, and then I think he said: "Well, that's that", or something very like it. I was really very upset myself about his disappointment, and I tried to explain how very costly it would have been to turn into flats, and how Mr. Buss thought they wouldn't be suitable anyway.'

'And how did he take that?'

'Very reasonably. He said he saw my point of view and that *I* mustn't feel badly about it. He said it was my house, after all, and I could do as I wished with it. But of course I didn't feel very happy about him.'

'No,' said Gabrielle, who did not feel happy about him either.

'I hope it doesn't mean that I won't see as much of him. He came to my rescue when my sisters died, giving me company and comfort when he needn't have done . . .'

Inevitably, however, it did mean that Ivor was less at Medlicott House. Gabrielle never met him there. She had no reason to ring him up, nor did he ring her. Several times she saw his car on the road. This was to be expected since he was constantly driving between Village and Cottage Hospital, Town and big hospital, and must have passed the Tudor Rose every day, often several times. Before, he had stopped his car to speak to Gabrielle if she was riding. Now he lifted a hand in salute and passed by. She was troubled about him, and so was Miss Medlicott.

She saw him at last when she was driving home through the Town from a cocktail party. He was emerging from the Town Hall with some other men, and then left to make for his car. Gabrielle hesitated about stopping, then braked and drew in to the kerb. The street, at this time of evening, was quiet and almost empty.

'Good evening, Ivor,' she said, as he drew near.

'Good evening, Gabrielle.' Unsmiling, quite serious.

What had she stopped for? What was there to say to him?

'What are *you* doing here?' was what she said, and at once it sounded impertinent to her, and she wished she could take it back.

'I've been to a Council meeting,' he said.

'You, on the Council, with all your other work to do?'

'The way to find out what's cooking, and the way to get my own ideas carried through is to be on the Council, parish and county. It's hard enough to sway events *on* the Council, impossible off it.'

She saw that there was a grim thrust to his jawline and wondered if he had tried to sway events this evening. For the first time she was embarrassed with him, and wished she had not stopped. But she wanted to mention the fact that Miss Medlicott missed him, and she could not speak to him like this, he aloof on the pavement and she peering up at him from the car. So she got out and stood beside him.

'Ivor, Miss Medlicott is a little upset because you don't go and see her now. Couldn't you spare her a moment now and then?'

'She doesn't need me now,' he said. 'I went because she was lonely and grieving for her sisters. Now she has a variety of interests. Joe Buss has got the bit between his teeth over that coachhouse of hers, and is always in and out. She has you. And your family.'

'But she thought you were her friend.'

'Good God, of *course* I'm her friend. I like her. But that doesn't mean I make time for her when she has other friends and interests. I've got other people to worry about.'

'She thinks it's because you were disappointed in her.'

There was a long pause.

'You mean she thinks I'm sulking. . . . Well, it isn't like that at all. All right, I'll go in and see her.'

'I'm not trying to manage your affairs, Ivor,' Gabrielle said with some hesitation.

'Aren't you? I thought that was what you *were* doing.'

'No, only trying to persuade you.'

'A gentler example of the same thing. And you're pretty good at persuasion, Gabrielle.'

'I don't know what that means,' she said stiffly.

'I think you do. You persuaded Miss Medlicott very successfully.'

'I did nothing of the kind! If you want to know who did the persuading you can look to your own friend, Joe Buss.'

'Joe Buss was working for me.'

'Until he saw the unsuitability of your scheme, and how perfect ours was.'

'And so you have your hotel,' he said.

'It isn't my hotel,' she exclaimed. 'It's my family's.'

'A distinction without a difference.'

There was another pause. Ivor looked the length of the uninteresting street. He made a movement of departure. Gabrielle said:

'I think I stopped with the idea of telling you how very sorry I was that your plan fell through. Obviously, one side had to be disappointed. But I was sorry.'

'The people to be sorry for are the people who might have lived there, and now won't. People who are eating their hearts out with loneliness.' He began to pace along the pavement and almost unconsciously she turned to pace with him. 'It's hard for you to understand, Gabrielle, and I don't blame you. Why should a girl who is young and beautiful, with work to do and friends all round her, be able to understand? I didn't understand myself, at first.'

They came to the bridge over the river and stopped to lean on the balustrade and look at the water beneath. They were almost unaware of the cars that swished behind them over the bridge. He said slowly, thoughtfully:

'When I started in practice, here with my father, it was

the dramatic in medicine and surgery that appealed to me. The crisis of life and death. The accident in the factory or pit or on the road – when I could do something concrete about it. Set the broken limbs, give blood transfusions, and morphia for the pain. Delivering babies in remote places with no amenities. Performing the emergency operation on a kitchen table.

'It took me a few years to get beyond this phase. To realize that this was the obvious and the easy, and to get down to the suffering that wasn't easy to locate, that might be longer lasting, even catastrophic. The nervous breakdown that must be due to *something*, the suicide that must have a cause, the severe asthma that resulted from a hopeless love affair.

'It was a further step still to appreciate the despair of loneliness, and to know that it has no limits of age or wealth. You've heard of cases, you must have done, where old people have died alone and perhaps nobody has discovered it for several days.

'It was for lonely people that I wanted Medlicott. So that they would have a neighbour. So that they would pass each other in the garden with a pleasant good-morning. So that their rooms would be warm, and they would have at least one good meal a day, and it wouldn't be possible for them to die in loneliness. Even, perhaps, so that I could see so many of them under one roof, and not drive a hundred miles between them all. A selfish reason, you see.

'They would have paid what they could afford to pay. Mrs. Barnes, next to nothing. Mrs. Gresham quite dearly. The most expensive school in England works on that principle. And I would have forced grants out of various authorities like blood out of a stone if necessary.

'But now a few lonely people who might have been rescued will go on being lonely. And you have your hotel.'

They walked back to the cars in complete silence. At her car, Gabrielle stopped.

'I suppose I shouldn't have said all that,' Ivor said.

'Of course you know that you've burdened me now with a terrible feeling of guilt,' Gabrielle replied.

'That will do no harm.' His voice was dry. 'If a few more people felt guilt, more might be done.'

He opened the car door for her and she got in.

'Give Miss Medlicott my love,' he said, 'and tell her I'll be along.'

'I will,' she said, and he closed her in.

'Good night, Gabrielle,' he said.

She nodded at him. And now it was she who was unsmiling. She drove homeward. When she left the cocktail party, she had been feeling gay and lighthearted. Now she was sober and thoughtful.

She did not think he was bitter. She thought he had accepted the verdict, knowing, from his experience of life, that most people were selfish through not realizing enough. The big disaster, the flood or earthquake, brought immediate responses: the day-to-day privations and suffering were not conspicuous, became a bore. Gabrielle imagined this was how he was thinking, and that she would be lumped in his mind with all the people who did not care.

Until now, he had counted on her sympathy: had said, with that hint of humour she had often seen (but certainly not tonight): 'I thought you might well have a soul to save.' And she had been angry. And had said, when she apologized to him: 'Ah shore do appreciate that, ma'am.' And later: 'All is forgiven and forgotten' with true melodrama. And he had even kissed her, very thoroughly, because, he had said, he could not resist women when they were angry. But why, really, had he kissed her, and with no half-measures?

She arrived at the Tudor Rose quiet and subdued, fairly

certain that Ivor was now thinking she had no soul to save. Her mother, noticing the slight despondency, said:

'Not a good party, Gay?' and Gabrielle had to recall herself to the present, having almost forgotten the cocktail party.

'Oh, not bad, Mama,' she said. 'Not bad.'

By the time Howard Nelmes arrived for a three-day weekend, Gabrielle had recovered her spirits. The hotel was full now and would remain full for the next two months, with a special influx of children during August. This was how the Knights liked it. It was probably one of the reasons for their success as hoteliers that, even during the busiest periods, they never flapped. Even the wedding receptions for which they were justly renowned were not refused during this busy time, although they sometimes made a great mess, with confetti and rose petals and silver horse-shoes. All the staff got together to restore things to normal, sweetened by the thought of the tips to come, kept in good humour because all the Knights worked too.

Howard, as usual, wanted to carry Gabrielle away.

'Impossible, Howard,' she said, shaking her head. 'We're much too busy. You must see that.'

'Let Mary take over at Reception.'

'She takes over so many other things that she can't do Reception too.'

'Yes, she can,' observed Catherine from farther along the counter. 'When *you* all move on to Medlicott, I'm keeping Mary as my receptionist. She's as keen as mustard. Hop off, Gay, and Mary can leave whatever she's doing and come to the desk.'

Gabrielle gave her aunt an accusing look. It seemed to her that the whole family pushed her into Howard's arms whenever possible. And very willing arms they were, waiting to receive her. They drove off, over the hills and far away, equipped with a special lunch and a bottle of wine.

'I'm off to Spain next week,' Howard said, as they sat with their picnic looking out over the rolling hills and the lakes.

'Ah yes,' Gabrielle remembered.

'Will you miss me?'

'Honestly, I'll be too busy, but I shall look forward to your coming back. You're staying with friends?'

'Yes. Do you know Spain?'

'No, it's not really one of my hunting grounds. I've been to Marbella for the sea, and Madrid . . .'

'You have to get off the beaten track in Spain. I shall be staying in a house not far from Granada − not that Granada's off the beaten track, of course; looking out over the whole dry Sierra de Nevada, which is. And you can still find the magic of Granada, you go at night when all the crowds have gone and you can have a guide to yourself, and all those courts are magically floodlit. . . . Come to Spain, Gay, for a few days at least.'

'What, now?'

'Yes. I'm sure your parents would spare you, and my friends would love to have you.'

'No,' she said, but smiled at him. 'Ask me another time, Howard, when it's not high season. I'm not playing at my job, and nobody else on the staff would dream of going away at this particular time. But it does sound heavenly.'

'It would be heavenly, Gay. Let's go somewhere, when your high season's over. When is that?'

'Towards the end of September, though we're fairly busy until the end of October − and open all the year round. Mother and Dad take a short break after October and then go off to Jamaica or the Bahamas for the whole of January. But my mother won't be able to tear herself away this year, if Medlicott is settled.'

'I shall like staying at Medlicott,' he said. 'The whole place appeals to me.'

'I know you have very extravagant tastes,' she teased him.

'I admit it. But it's not for the fleshpots. I like beautiful things. Like you,' he added, taking the hand that held her wineglass and kissing it.

'Only for my beauty? Not for my kind nature?'

'For everything about you, Gay.'

'I don't think you know everything about me yet.'

'No. That's one of the interesting things, finding out.'

'Let's hope you don't find out too many dark and secret places,' she said, laughing at him.

'But that would be interesting, too,' he declared.

Dark and secret places, she thought, and wondered if there were any in his life. He seemed pleasant and open, he had a great deal of charm, but he was also a successful businessman, so must at times be ruthless too. He liked to fish and shoot and play golf, all the acceptable things; he collected various kinds of antiques, glass paperweights from Clichy and Baccarat, and the sort of French Louis furniture that cost a fortune. He was, she thought, a conformist, but there was nothing wrong with that.

It was Ivor Huwlett who came into her mind with the phrase 'dark and secret places' for she felt sure they were hidden in *his* nature. She thought he might well be moody, sometimes despairing of human nature itself, sometimes despondent about his failures, or obsessed by difficult cases, or even caught up in the darkness of other people's lives.

Gabrielle and Howard did not reach the hotel until after six o'clock. Already the courtyard was full of cars, as people arrived for the bars, or residents returned from a day out or an afternoon drive; to rest or change, or put their children to bed before dinner. It was a time of the day that Gabrielle liked. One was aware that something was going on behind all those doors: children turbulent in baths, older people somnolent in them. Dresses being taken from wardrobes and inspected, beads or jewellery chosen to accompany them; men shaving for the second time that day; mothers hurrying children, men kissing their wives. And very shortly, the early diners coming downstairs for a drink in the lounge before dinner, or in the bar.

Most people still changed for dinner, although the men might wear fine roll-collar jerseys of coral or green or yellow under their jackets, or flowery shirts or lace ones. The girls and women liked to dress and make-up and show off their finery. Gabrielle, often at her desk at this time, with a smile and a word for everybody, was interested in the evening pageant.

On this particular evening, some miles away, returning from the big hospital to the Town, and then towards the lake, Ivor Huwlett braked his car as Nurse Harper thumbed a lift from him, and, opening the door for her, said:

'What happened to *you*?'

'Breakdown,' she said. 'I had to leave my car at the Clinic; and not a taxi to be had anywhere. There never is in this benighted place! I got a lift as far as this; and am I glad to see you!'

'You sound fed up.'

'Yes, I am.'

'Heavy day, Pat?'

'Not more than usual. It's just me, I suppose.'

'You need a holiday.'

'Like all of us! Where's the money coming from?'

'Oh my, you *are* blue!'

'Can't seem to shake myself out of it. Take no notice of me, Ivor.'

'What are you doing this evening?'

'Nothing. That means eating with my parents, getting a breath of air in the garden, seeing if there's anything to watch on TV.'

'You need a drink,' he said. 'The evil stimulus of alcohol.'

'I need several,' she said.

'Right. Several you shall have.' He drove past her parents' house towards the lake.

'Hi, where are we going, Ivor?'

'To the Tudor Rose.'

'But you never go there!'

'We're going there tonight. My mother's away and I don't feel like going back to an empty house.'

There was nowhere to park on the courtyard. Ivor swept round to the back of the hotel, where a Rolls kept company with an E-type Jaguar and a superb Bentley. 'Mixing with our betters,' he said, helping Pat out of the car.

They went into the saloon bar and took the small table of two people leaving for the dining-room. They sank into the comfortable chairs with relief.

'This looks cosy,' said Ivor, glancing round the big room.

'I wish I didn't look so nursey,' said Pat.

'You look fine, Pat.'

'When I've had a couple of drinks to revive me, I'll go and clean up,' she said.

The drinks revived them both.

'Sorry if I grizzled, Ivor. I feel better now.'

'You'll feel better still with a good dinner inside you. We'll have it here.'

'Hurrah,' said Pat. 'Luxury, for once.'

'Wait until they open Medlicott House. *That* will be luxury for you. I'll take you there, you shall be one of the first to dine there.'

'I'll hold you to that, Ivor, but I'll manage to make do with this this evening.'

It seemed, however, that even this was to be denied her. They came to the entrance to the dining-room to be met with a regretful refusal from Pierre, the head waiter. Pierre, who was Peter in his private life, also had plans for Medlicott House and saw himself there as maître d'hôtel, at least.

Gabrielle, leaving the desk to go to the private room, saw Pierre turning somebody away, and next moment realized, with a shock, that that person was Ivor Huwlett. She went immediately to his side.

'Ivor,' she said. 'How nice to see you here.'

'But you can't give us dinner.'

'Of course we can,' she said at once. 'Pierre!'

'We are quite full, Miss Gay, and several reservations still to come.'

'But we must find a place for Dr. Huwlett,' she said. 'We are honoured to have him. Can't you arrange something, Pierre?'

Pierre knew that he had to arrange something. 'I will see what can be done,' he offered.

'If you would wait just a moment, Ivor . . .'

'Thank you,' he said stiffly. 'Gabrielle, this is Pat Harper, who spends half her time being my indispensable nurse. Pat, perhaps you've met Miss Knight.'

The two young women said good evening to each other. Pierre had called two young waiters to bring in an extra table and they were busy covering it with a snow-white cloth, cutlery and flowers.

'Would you like a drink while you are waiting?' asked Gabrielle.

'I've already had too many, thank you,' said Pat.

Gabrielle gave them her most dazzling smile.

'Then if you will excuse me,' she said, preparing to leave. 'I hope you will enjoy your dinner.' She saw that Pierre himself showed them to their table, unfolded their napkins to put across their laps, offered them the menu. Then he joined her outside in the wide passage.

'The best dinner the Rose can produce,' she said to him. 'And their wine with the compliments of the management.'

'Certainly, Miss Gay,' he said, wondering why two tired-looking people who had not bothered to change merited this special treatment.

'This *is* nice,' said Pat, looking about her. 'I wish you'd given me time to change, though.'

'If I can eat in these clothes, sweetie, you can eat in those,' he told her.

'An uncomprehending barbarian,' she said, shaking her head.

'Such long words, Pat. Too much for my tired brain. Let's have a gorgeous dinner.'

They had their gorgeous dinner. They were gratified at the quality of the wine the management refused to let them pay for. Ivor said the Tudor Rose certainly did one well, unaware that the very best quality, the very best service had been ordered for them.

'Too well,' said Pat. 'D'you know, Ivor, I don't believe I'm going to make it to the car. The drinks before dinner, the wine with it, I'm feeling kind of giddy . . .'

'Honestly?'

'Honestly. I'm wondering if my legs are going to hold me up.'

He smiled at her.

'You haven't drunk *that* much, Pat. But don't worry, I shall support you. People will simply think that we're a very close couple.'

I wish we were, thought Pat. She waited while Ivor came round the table and pulled back her chair for her, helping her considerately to her feet. He tucked an arm firmly under hers. 'O.K.?' he asked her softly.

'So far,' she whispered back, feeling an unusual tendency to giggle.

She made her escape with dignity. They crossed the lounge hall arm in arm, Pat's head inclining towards Ivor's shoulder. 'The fresh air,' he whispered, bending his head down to hers, 'will either make you or break you.' The words did not make much sense to Pat, but fortunately the fresh air did not prove to be her undoing. She stood breathing it in for a few seconds and already felt better.

'I'm going to run you back to my house,' he said, 'to give you something to put you right; and then I'll take you home.'

Gabrielle, who had finished dinner long before Ivor and Pat, saw them leave. She thought, as Ivor had intended other people should think, that they seemed a very close couple. They were almost embracing as they crossed the hall, the girl's head almost on Ivor's shoulder. Gabrielle also noticed that they had not changed, and wondered if they had been working long, arduous hours together. She wondered further what it would be like to work with Ivor Huwlett day after day. She stood for some time gazing absently at the door that had closed behind them, following them in fancy to – where?

Why had she always thought of him as a solitary person, simply because when she met him, he was usually alone? This had been his home all his life, he was known by almost everybody, he probably had an immense circle of friends. Why had she never thought of him in connection with other women? Just because he had not yet married, it did not mean that there were not many women who would like to marry him. The one he was with now, for instance . . .

Catherine was suddenly beside her.

'They tell me,' said her indignant voice, 'that Dr. Huwlett was here to dinner. Can you imagine such impertinence? And that *you*, Gay, ordered a bottle of your father's best claret for them on the house. How could you?'

'Oh, really, Aunt Catherine,' Gabrielle said impatiently, 'isn't it about time you buried that old hatchet?' and she walked quickly away along the wide passage to the kitchens.

'Well!' exclaimed Catherine, deflated, watching her go, thinking: 'What's got into her, to make her so irritable?'

CHAPTER SIX

HIGH season was over. It had been a good season, but everybody on the staff of the Tudor Rose was tired after it. Casual staff was kept on while regular members took holidays during October and November, most of them flying off to places where the sun still shone. Mr. and Mrs. Knight went to the Canary Islands for ten days and returned invigorated, and Catherine departed for Crete.

Gabrielle unexpectedly found herself with time on her hands and nobody to help her use it.

Howard, who had returned from Spain with plans for a holiday for her, had been sent to the Far East. Ivor was no more than a hand that waved briefly to her from a car in passing. He did not come again to the Tudor Rose, he made no effort to see her, and she found that as she saw him less, she thought of him proportionately more.

There were always some people staying in the hotel, but most of the bedrooms were empty. The restaurant did good business but was no longer crowded. The bars were always lively and well patronized. But Gabrielle had not enough to do.

'I'd forgotten how quiet it is here at this time of year,' she said to her parents, as they dined at their leisure.

'You haven't been here at this time for many years,' said her mother. 'Even when you were away at school, you came home at the end of term to all the excitement of Christmas.'

'Which will be our next big event,' said Mr. Knight.

'Why, are you bored, Gay?'

'No, not bored, I can catch up on all the books I want to

read; but I could do with more work.'

'My dear, you can help me with Medlicott! That will give us plenty to do. I've come back from holiday dying to get on with the organization of that.'

'The sale hasn't been completed, has it?'

'No, but we don't expect any hitch, and Miss Medlicott has agreed to our getting started. I've got Tommy Davenport as our architect – I think he's brilliant. I had thought of Jonathan Scott,' (whose name was a famous one throughout the country) 'but he seemed so busy and rather patronizing, consenting to squeeze us in between other jobs, that I'm sure we wouldn't get enough attention from him.'

'And Tommy is a good public relations man,' said Mr. Knight.

'Yes, he'll get us into gossip columns and the glossies. As a matter of fact,' said Mrs. Knight, slightly embarrassed by her own forward-thinking, 'he took some beautiful colour pictures of the grounds for me in the spring when all the rhodos and azaleas were in bloom, showing the lake and the swans *et al.*'

Gabrielle smiled at her.

'Your incurable optimism!' she said.

'Well, even if we hadn't got the place, the pictures would have been nice to have. As it is, they will whet people's appetites. So you see, Gay, there'll be plenty for you to do. We'll go to London and choose materials for curtains and bedcovers, carpets where necessary – oh, thousands of things. Miss Medlicott is quite willing for us to go over the house whenever we choose.'

'She's so wrapped up in her own new house,' Gabrielle said. 'It seems that every time I go there Joe Buss is with her discussing it. The garden boundary has been demarcated, her garage is already built, and the house is coming along at an astonishing rate; which shows what can be done when the builder has a soft spot for one.'

Gabrielle had been, in fact, a little put out by Miss Medlicott's dependence on Mr. Buss, which made her feel slightly *de trop*. It seemed to her that he was at Medlicott House more often than his work required, and there was often a hurried rolling up of plans when Gabrielle arrived that smacked of secrecy and of excluding her.

Mrs. Knight had measured coffee into the pot and switched it on. While coffee was making, Mr. Knight went out to see that all was well in the lounge hall, the sitting-room and the bars. He came back in a few minutes.

'Everybody as snug as a bug in a rug,' he commented.

His words suddenly diverted the trend of Gabrielle's thoughts. It always was snug in the Tudor Rose with its leaping fires added to the central heating. Guests loved an open fire and invariably gathered round these focal spots. Startling contrasts presented themselves to Gabrielle. Her imagination saw a picture of the outside world; darkness coming in early, mists hiding the tops of the hills and drifting down into the valleys: solitary, isolated homes surrounded by the mist, quiet, cut off, no visitors during the long, dark evenings.

Mrs. Barnes, for instance. Was she back, after her fall, in her little house under the cliff surrounded by the stunted trees? And Mrs. Gresham, sitting among her treasures, missing her husband and listening to the wind in the chimney. And the woman up in the quarry, where all the slate would be glistening grey in the damp – had she had her sixth child yet? What a place to bring a new and helpless baby into!

Suddenly she realized that if she had time on her hands, there was a use to which she could put it.

She started with Mrs. Barnes. She was given a warm welcome and offered tea. Already the mist was drifting past as Gabrielle went inside, and the house was definitely chilly:

no central heating here. But the sitting-room was so small that it was adequately heated by the coal fire. Gabrielle had taken cakes and home-made bread from the Tudor Rose kitchens, and they had tea together.

She offered to do any shopping necessary, and Mrs. Barnes said:

'Well, there is one grocer who still comes up from the Village once a week, and he brings my little bit of meat from the butcher; and if a penny or two goes on everything, well, he's got his petrol and van to pay for, and it's worth it. But what I really need is a couple of new nighties, and he can't very well choose those for me.'

So a shopping expedition was organized for Mrs. Barnes. Not in the Town, with its new shops, but in the Village, where the poky little draper's shop produced the right night-dresses, and where Mrs. Barnes enjoyed lengthy conversations with all the shopkeepers who knew her. 'That was a *real* treat,' she said as she thanked Gabrielle; left once more in her lonely hillside retreat.

It was to the quarry that Gabrielle next went, riding Chestnut because she did not trust herself to get a car safely up that hazardous road. When she saw the state of the road as she emerged from the wood to the uplands, she was glad of her choice. Half of the road had become a stream racing downhill, and there seemed to be more boulders than ever scattering the broken surface.

When she reached the row of dilapidated cottages, she thought they were all abandoned. There was no sign of life anywhere. Perhaps the families had been turned out by the authorities. She was about to turn away again when she saw two of the children peering at her through a window. She turned back. The woman opened the door to her reluctantly.

Gabrielle was appalled at the intense cold inside, and

although all the children were bundled into as many old clothes and rags as could be found, they all looked pinched. This time the woman was too miserable even to be suspicious, and succumbed to all Gabrielle's questions. Gabrielle, looking at the lined, worn face, realized that she must once have been pretty, with fine dark eyes. She was heavily pregnant and admitted that the child should be born in about a week's time.

'But not here?' asked Gabrielle.

'I don't know where else,' said the woman.

'Have you got help?'

'No. *She*,' indicating by a movement of the head the other cottage that had been inhabited, 'went away with her old man when it got cold. There's on'y us now.'

'Where's your husband?'

'Well, 'e went away to get some work and a bit o' cash. 'E ain't never left me yet when one o' the kids was due.'

'Can't Dr. Huwlett get you into the Cottage Hospital? Would your husband look after the children?'

'I ain't 'avin' no truck with 'ospitals. They'd split us up. They done it before. Sid in one place, and me with two o' the kids in another, and the boy somewhere else. They're never goin' ter split us up agin.'

She can't stay here, thought Gabrielle. No fuel. Next to no food. I shall simply have to do something for them myself.

There was the sound of an engine labouring up the rough hillside. The children rushed to the window, and the woman looked alarmed for a moment before her face cleared. 'It's the doctor,' she said; and from the tone of her voice it was as if God himself had leaned from Heaven to help her.

Gabrielle looked out of the window as well. Ivor had jumped out and opened the back of the Land-Rover. He was wearing a fine, warm sheepskin coat and the ridiculous bobble hat. He unloaded a couple of heavy sacks and humped the first one to the battered doorway.

'Hallo, everybody,' he said. 'Here's something to keep you warm. A sack of coal and a sack of logs. Come on, Bobby, let's see you light a fire. There's newspaper in the car and here's some matches. Catch!' The boy caught the matches, his face split into a huge smile. 'Well, Mrs. Sanders, you're still in one piece, I see.' Suddenly he caught sight of Gabrielle, standing in the shadowy background. 'What's this?' he asked. 'A ministering angel? Are there such things any more?' He didn't wait to be answered, but turned back to the woman. 'I want to take a look at you,' he said. 'As soon as we've brought some stuff from the car. Come on, all of you, come and lend a hand.'

The children poured out of the house around him. Gabrielle went too. Two boxes containing groceries and bread and milk. A heap of clothes. 'My mother's been round the jumble sales,' he said to Gabrielle. Everything was carried inside. The children immediately began to sort out the clothes, coats, sweaters, socks, Wellington boots. 'Got the whole lot for a few shillings,' Ivor said to the woman, 'and my mother's scouting round now for baby clothes. We'll set you up all right.'

He turned to the children. 'Out,' he said. 'Into the back kitchen, the lot of you. I want to have a look at your mother.' Gabrielle went with them, and was appalled again by the back kitchen; its open hearth with a couple of cheap and blackened pots; the lack of any sink, stove, or any sort of amenity; bleak, dark stone walls.

When Ivor was ready to leave, Gabrielle went too.

They stood together surrounded by boulders and fallen walls and glistening grey slate.

'Housing is the problem?' said Gabrielle.

'Yes, they don't stand a chance of a council house; they

can't pay the rents asked nowadays, and who'd let even a third-rate place to a couple with six children? They were split up before into various institutions, and the idea fills them with dread.' He looked down at Gabrielle. 'I've put myself absolutely in the wrong, of course, by not reporting them as squatters up here. Quite a few people know about them, but nobody has reported them. I don't want to split them up, it would break her heart. But after this child, I'll see to it that she doesn't have any more.'

'She isn't going to have her baby in there, is she?'

'No, I've got her a bed in the Cottage Hospital. She'll raise hell, I daresay. If her husband comes back, he can look after the children. If not, my mother will do some scouting round for them.'

'Will the husband come back, Ivor?'

'He hasn't deserted her yet when her children were born. But this one must be the last. They started out with high hopes, you know, and the hope has been slowly squeezed out of them, and now they only have despair.'

'And you,' she said.

He gave her an intent look.

'Well, what were *you* doing there?' he asked.

'I was curious about what was happening to them.'

'Only curious?'

'Concerned. A bit worried.'

'That's better. . . . You're riding down, I see.'

'Yes, I wasn't brave enough to come up in a car.'

'Thank goodness you weren't. You need a Land-Rover or a tractor, and then you spin all over the place. Take care, Gabrielle, going down.'

'I will,' she said.

He made no move to go. He still stood beside her, looking down at her with a kind and approving smile – almost affectionate. He said:

'We don't want anything to happen to you.'

'You wouldn't want me as a patient?' she asked, smiling.

'Would *you* want *me* as a doctor?'

'Oh, I'm sure I could do a lot worse,' she assured him.

'Well, anyway, look after yourself. Take care.'

He did go, then. She watched his Land-Rover dodging about to avoid the larger boulders. She rode home, realizing how much more welcoming and temperate it was in the valley than up on those bare hills. She returned Chestnut to his stable, drove home and found her parents at lunch.

'Sorry to be late,' she said, joining them. 'Dad, you remember that cottage in the hollow?'

'Hm-mmm.'

'What are you going to do with it?'

'Jim and Millie moved in there yesterday.'

'Oh, damn! Well, what about the cottage they've left?'

'I've told the Willises who've got that caravan along by the river that they can have it for a month. He goes off to a new job then with a tied cottage. Too cold in their caravan now.'

'What a nuisance!' exclaimed Gabrielle.

'Why are you so interested?'

'I wanted it to keep a family together until something else can be thought out for them.'

'It's not fit to live in, Gay.'

'It was good enough for Jim all those years.'

'No bathroom, loo outside the back door, roof wants attention, the rain comes in the smallest bedroom, brick floor in the kitchen inclined to be damp.'

'What *you* call not fit to live in, Dad! It would be a paradise for this family.' She told them about the family squatting in the quarry cottage.

'The man's probably a no-good,' said her father.

124

'Drop-outs from society,' said Mrs. Knight.

Gabrielle thought: That's how I might have seen it a little while ago, and said:

'I want to help that woman. Ivor says this couple started out with high hopes and now they have only despair.'

'Who's Ivor?' asked her father.

'Ivor Huwlett, of course.'

'So that's what this is all about. *He* wants you to get the cottage for them.'

'He doesn't know a thing about it. I just happened to ride up that way when I first came home and met him up there. He'd been operating on the boy for appendicitis: up in that awful place. . . . Well, can I have it, Dad, when these Willises move on?'

'All right, please yourelf. They'll probably break all the windows and tear the place apart.'

'Thank you, Dad. But I *did* hope they'd be installed somewhere before this baby pops out.'

Gabrielle thought she might just get them in by Christmas. Out in the old barn there was a great deal of furniture rejected by the hotel, knocked-about tables and chairs, old beds, pieces of carpet too worn for guests' bedrooms. She could raid the kitchen for battered pots and pans, odd pieces of china. There were even toys, games and books which were used by child guests when the weather was bad: some of these could go to the cottage too.

She wanted to ring up Ivor and tell him this piece of good news; but she found herself shy these days of using the telephone to him, because he might once more be in the middle of something important. So she wrote a letter about it, saying that Mrs. Sanders might be reconciled to going to hospital if she could give a proper address for herself and her children; and that from this address the older children would be able to go to school. His reply was surely the shortest letter she had ever received. It said: 'A ministering angel, indeed! Thank you. Ivor.'

She was not sure if this pleased her or not, but as she was left with an odd sense of loss that persisted for some time, she came to the conclusion that it did not.

On a cold, raw evening of December with a fine sleet falling over the dark countryside, the saloon bar of the Tudor Rose was more welcoming than ever, well lit, warmly carpeted, a fine fire leaping in the open grate. It was crowded because a dance was being held in the long room at the side of the Tudor Rose; and because the dance was to celebrate the birthday of one of her friends, Gabrielle was in the bar too, having a drink with early arrivals, dressed in a green dress which accentuated her golden hair and rose-petal skin. It was a simple dress, given glamour by the embroidery scattered over it, heightened by glistening beads and pearl drops. There were so many beautiful dresses there that Pat Harper was noticeable when she appeared in the bar in her navy blue raincoat and neat, dark hat. Gabrielle noticed that she also wore Wellington boots.

Pat went to the bar and spoke to Tony, the barman. Tony shook his head. She obviously pressed him, because Tony looked thoughtfully at her, only to shake his head again. Gabrielle excused herself to her friends and went to Pat's side.

'Good evening, Miss Harper, can I help you?'

'I hope you can,' said Pat's worried voice. 'My car's broken down and I'm on my way to a case. I wondered if you had a taxi or hotel transport or something.'

'Where do you want to go?' asked Gabrielle, shepherding Pat away from the bar.

'Well, that's just it. I'm supposed to meet Dr. Huwlett at the gate to the wood, so that he can take me up to the quarry. There's a woman up there going to have a baby . . .'

'Yes, I know about it.'

'But because of this breakdown, I'm so late that he might have gone on. That damned car! It's let me down several times lately and I can't get a new one out of the authorities. Do you think you *could* help?'

'I would drive you to the gate in my car, but it wouldn't go up that awful road at the top.'

'Then I've let him down,' said Pat, and her voice was despairing.

'Wouldn't he wait for you?'

'For a while perhaps, then he'd go on. The eldest child had to run down the hillside to get him, and he rang me; so God knows what's happening up there.'

'All right,' said Gabrielle. 'You can have the hotel van. It got up there in the summer.'

Pat was obviously scared stiff at the thought of taking an unknown van, considerably larger than her own small car, up that ruined road. Gabrielle said on impulse: 'I'll come with you. If Dr. Huwlett is waiting at the gate, I can come back. If not, we'll chance it together.'

Pat looked at Gabrielle's beautiful dress.

'You're going somewhere,' she said.

'There's a dance right here. I can come back to it.'

'Would you have a couple of old blankets? I brought my bag, but had to leave the blankets in the car. And a small bottle of brandy? Ivor's sure to have some, but just in case.'

Gabrielle asked Tony to see to that. She put on a warm, midi-length sheepskin coat, a suede cap and Wellington boots, and thus incongruously dressed, set out with Pat.

She began to explain the gears of the van to Pat.

'Oh, would you drive?' asked Pat. 'You know the vehicle much better than I do.' So Gabrielle got into the driving seat, and with Pat beside her set off for the gate into the wood.

The doctor was not there.

'He'll have gone up long ago,' said Pat.

Gabrielle's heart sank at the thought of driving up to the quarry. The sleet falling was just enough to blur one's vision. The windscreen wipers made small piles of it on the bonnet of the van. She remembered the road, but memory made it no less cruel: the bends on the steepest part, the boulders that had to be avoided, the water rushing down that made a mud bed in which wheels slipped and skidded.

She screwed her courage to the sticking point, set her face in a grim, determined mask, and drove up through the wood. Pat, beside her, hung on with both hands, exclaiming involuntarily when the wheels skidded, filled with anxiety when it seemed the van would not labour up the steep and slippery slope – an anxiety that communicated itself to Gabrielle and added to her own. They bumped and jarred over smaller boulders that Gabrielle saw too late through the sleet, they went into a long skid that it seemed to take them an eternity to get out of, and Gabrielle remembered the few places in which a longish skid might take them to the edge of a sheer drop.

The road seemed twice as long as it had in summer. If there had been another path, Gabrielle would have thought they had gone wrong. As it was, she plodded on, not convinced that they would arrive at the derelict cottage without accident.

Then they saw the lights of the Land-Rover, directed full on to the house; with the intention, no doubt, of shedding extra light into that dismal room. The glimmer from the house itself they saw afterwards. Gabrielle drew the van to a stop, switched off the engine, and flopped her head down on to her arms on the steering wheel.

Pat was already out of the van, saying: 'You were marvellous, marvellous!' pulling out the blankets and her bag. Gabrielle was trembling violently, and her face was aching because of the intensity with which she had been gritting her teeth. It took her several minutes to recover herself. Then she followed Pat into the house.

The children had been pushed out into the back kitchen. Ivor and Pat were busy at the makeshift bed. As Gabrielle entered, Pat looked up at her briefly.

'Too late,' she said. 'We can't get her to the hospital in time.'

'What can I do?' asked Gabrielle.

Ivor looked up at her and saw that she was pale and still unsteady.

'You can take a good pull at the brandy bottle,' he said, 'and then leave us here and keep an eye on the infants out there.'

Gabrielle did as she was told. She left them to their mysteries and found the children scared and purposeless in the dreary little back kitchen. There was a candle in a recess in the wall.

'Why didn't you make a fire, Bobby?' she asked cheerfully.

'There ain't no chopped wood, miss. I told Mum I could use the axe, but she won't let me.'

'Perhaps I could chop some,' said Gabrielle doubtfully, and was horrified to see the size of the axe this small boy proposed to use. She managed to use it herself somewhat inefficiently and they made a blaze on the open hearth with newspaper and wood, which cheered them all; but it seemed to Gabrielle a long time before she heard the cry of a baby exercising its lungs for the first time. A little later, the door, hung on one rusty hinge, was pushed back and Pat's voice said cheerfully:

'Well, he's arrived. A baby brother for you all. He's a fine big, beautiful boy.'

'And Mrs. Sanders?' asked Gabrielle.

'Fine too.' Pat was practical now, all nurse-like efficiency. 'She's so used to it by now, I do believe she'd have got through it without us. Come and see him,' she invited the children, and they went through into the other room.

Gabrielle thought she would never forget this scene. Everybody was so happy. Mrs. Sanders gave them all a broad smile, holding the new arrival in her arms. The children crowded round the bed, touching the baby's cheek with their none-too-clean fingers. Ivor was making tea in a battered pot from a black kettle perched on the fire, and Pat was clearing up. The lights of the Land-Rover cast a garish glow over the dark stone walls, a cold and unearthly light. The chattering of the children was like the twittering of birds. They were excited about the new baby. Of course they must never be split up.

The first cup of tea went to Mrs. Sanders.

'I'll give you half an hour,' said Ivor, 'and then I'm taking you down to the Cottage Hospital. And don't argue,' before the poor woman could get out a word. 'Everything is settled. The children are going down to my mother for the time being. Tea, Pat. Gabrielle.' They stood around, drinking the hot, weak tea. 'Well, Mrs. Sanders, what are you going to call him?'

'Ivor,' she said at once.

'Now, you don't have to do that.'

'I wouldn't dream of calling 'im anything else,' she said. 'I on'y 'ope 'e'll turn out as good as you are.'

'Hear, hear,' said Pat, and smiled at Ivor and he smiled slowly back at her; and suddenly Gabrielle felt out in the cold, a stranger to them; hardly touching their lives which had so much in common. Theirs was a warm and understanding comradeship.

She stood sipping her hot tea, and her coat fell open in front, so that the embroidery on her dress glittered in the lights. One of the little girls stood in front of her, not daring to touch, fascinated by her glimpse of this beautiful dress. The grown-ups smiled at the expression on her face. Gabrielle opened her coat wider for the child's benefit.

'Isn't that pretty?' she said, smiling at the child.

The child nodded dumbly.

'Why, it isn't a ministering angel after all,' said Ivor's voice. 'It's a fairy godmother.'

'Is it really?' asked one of the children, and Ivor found himself involved in difficult explanations – which served him right, Gabrielle decided.

Her half-hour's rest finished, Mrs. Sanders was carefully wrapped up in the blankets Gabrielle had brought and carried out to the Land-Rover by Ivor. Pat carried out the baby; and the two-year-old, who cried at being thus deserted, was taken in the Land-Rover as well. When they were settled, Ivor came back to Gabrielle.

'I have to leave a note in a conspicuous position in case husband returns,' he said, and did so while Gabrielle and the other children waited. 'Now,' he said, 'can you manage to get these other children down the hillside and to my mother's house? My mother's expecting them.'

'Well, I just hope so,' she said on a short sigh. 'I was scared stiff coming up.'

'It will be easier going down,' he assured her. 'Take it easy, in low gear. I'll go first and you can follow my lights.'

The children were put in the van and Ivor closed them in securely. He turned to Gabrielle. Sleet settled on them softly. They were in darkness at the back of the van. 'O.K.?' he asked. 'Not really frightened?'

'Well, I wouldn't say that,' she said doubtfully.

'You're a good, brave girl,' he said, and put his arms around her. Gabrielle thought he was about to kiss her and pulled back sharply.

'A short while ago I was a fairy godmother,' she said sharply. 'A sarcasm I didn't appreciate.'

'My dear girl, I didn't mean to be sarcastic. As far as these children are concerned, you are a fairy godmother. You wave your wand and they get a cottage to live in . . .'

'There you are! You make it all sound so damned easy,' she cried, protesting.

'Well, we haven't got time to fight it out now,' he said. 'I've got a patient to get to hospital. Come along, get in, Gabrielle, everybody's waiting.'

'And they'd be waiting still if I hadn't struggled to get this van up here,' she retorted.

'I doubt it,' he said. 'I'd have managed somehow, and we'd have squeezed everybody into the Land-Rover.'

'You make me sorry I made the effort,' she said, and climbed into the van to drive the children down the hill.

He hesitated as if he would take her up on these words, then went forward to the Land-Rover and set off slowly down the hill.

Either it *was* easier going down or she was fortified by the presence of Ivor and the other vehicle, because the journey seemed shorter and easier. Ivor got out to open the woodland gate and to close it when both vehicles had gone through; and then he and Pat sped off to the cottage hospital and Gabrielle stopped at the doctor's house.

Mrs. Huwlett was pleased to see her again and pressed her to stay for a cup of coffee. They took the children into the big, warm kitchen, where they were able to shed some of those jumble-sale clothes, and sat them up at the table to bowls of soup and sandwiches. 'Then, I think, a good bath for them all,' said Ivor's mother, 'and bed.'

'You aren't going to keep them all?' asked Gabrielle.

'I haven't decided yet. I have friends who would take one or two, but I don't really feel they should be separated. Coffee, Miss Knight, and you'd better take off that warm coat.'

Gabrielle did so and was revealed in her beautiful dress surmounted by her suede cap and scarcely set off by the Wellington boots. They laughed at the picture she presented. 'It's a wonderful dress,' said Mrs. Huwlett, wishing that Ivor would sometimes be more frivolous than he was.

'There's a dance at the Tudor Rose. I ought to be getting back.'

'I would have kept you for supper, except for your dance, and the job of bathing all these children. Another time, perhaps?'

'I should enjoy that.'

'As it is, I expect Ivor will bring Pat in. Poor girl, I'm afraid her mealtimes are as unpredictable as Ivor's.'

Suddenly Gabrielle was glad she was otherwise engaged. It sounded as if Pat was a regular and welcome visitor. She herself had seen Ivor and Pat at the Tudor Rose, dining together, and leaving wrapped in each other's arms. She had seen that slow, warm smile exchanged between them this evening. She did not want to sit by and watch them again. She said good-bye to the children and went back to her dance.

Several times during the rest of the evening, however, she paused in wonderment at the contrast that evening had presented. She found that it was not of the utter bleakness of that quarry cottage that she thought, but of the happiness that had permeated the place when the children gathered round the new baby: Mrs. Sanders glowing, the children twittering. The glow wouldn't last. One knew that. But it had been there.

This was another world. Silks and chiffons and glowing colours. Jewels, real and otherwise, which gleamed and sparkled in the light. Cultured voices calling to each other. Champagne flowing, and gaiety that increased into the small hours, when they began to leave in their low sports cars, their elegant saloon cars. Appointments casually made for dinner or dinks. 'Do come, Gay!' 'Gay, darling . . .' 'Gay, my poppet!'

Everybody agreed that the Tudor Rose had done them proud. Gay undressed and got thankfully into her warm and comfortable bed.

At the same time, Ivor was getting sleepily out of his. An old man, who had been sent home to the Village after an operation, had suddenly collapsed. Ivor reached the bedside in time to see the old man die.

'We're sorry, doctor,' the son and daughter-in-law said, 'to have brought you out. We thought there was a chance, you see.'

'You did perfectly right,' Ivor assured them. 'But now there's nothing you can do until morning. Go to bed and try to sleep.'

He went home again, hoping that nothing more would happen that night to disturb his sleep.

The following day, Mr. and Mrs. Knight and Gabrielle went to lunch with Miss Medlicott. The view down to the lake was now grey and misty and pleasure was to be found inside the house instead of out; a fire burning in the drawing-room to add cosiness to central heating. Vases on pedestals held superb arrangements of chrysanthemums.

Mr. and Mrs. Knight were to spend the afternoon in a further reconnaissance of the house. Gabrielle was taken to see the progress of the coachhouse conversion.

'It is almost ready, Gabrielle. Mr. Buss's men have been astonishingly quick. And there seems to be nothing that Mr.

Buss cannot find. He has been twice to London on my behalf, and brought so many samples of wallpaper and fabrics and door furniture that I've been hard put to it to make a selection.'

'But you're going to have a lovely house.'

'Yes, I think so. He tells me I shall be able to move in in the New Year, and I shall bring over all I need from Medlicott, and your parents will be able to make their selection from the rest. Anything they don't want can go to be auctioned.'

'Has Mr. Buss persuaded you to make that vista down to the lake?'

'No, we have changed out minds about that.' Gabrielle noticed that 'we'. 'But some trees between the coachhouse and the lake will go, so that I can see the water. And Mr. Buss has cleverly arranged a terrace for me, screened at one end from the wind, and quite private. Yet from my small sitting-room, I shall be able to see what is going on on the terrace of the big house.'

'Mr. Buss will miss Medlicott when his work here is finished.'

'I don't think so. He has a bigger job to get on with, when this is finished.'

'Won't *you* miss your discussions with him?'

'I rather think I may still be involved, since he seems to value my opinion on various matters.'

Gabrielle thought it had been obvious from the first that Mr. Buss had a very soft spot for Miss Medlicott. It couldn't be that romance was brewing in that quarter? No, the idea was ridiculous. And it couldn't be his interest in her considerable fortune? No, she did not think that the right answer either. It must be pure friendship, she decided.

It was dark when they returned to the Tudor Rose.

'I shall go on thinking of this as "home" for years,' Mrs.

Knight said as they went into the large hall. 'It will seem strange to preside at Medlicott.' She paused, as a tall man rose from an armchair where he had obviously been waiting for them. 'Why, look who's here!' she said delightedly, but Gabrielle did not need enlightening. She had gone forward with both hands outstretched to greet Howard, who took the hands to pull her into his arms and give her a hug.

Everybody was pleased to see him. They adjourned to the private room where the usual good fire awaited them, and Mr. Knight poured drinks for them all.

'Are you back for good?' Gabrielle asked him.

'No, I've flown home for Christmas,' he said.

'But that's still two weeks away!'

'Yes. I'm taking a month, and then I have to go back for a short spell. I'll have to put in a certain amount of time at the office while I'm in England; that's unavoidable. But I intend a lot of my time to be spent here.'

He had brought back beautiful eastern silks in glowing colours for Gabrielle, Mrs. Knight and Catherine too. And for Gabrielle, two birds in jade, so beautiful that Gabrielle was entranced, and so expensive that her parents exchanged glances as they pondered on Howard's motives. Mrs. Knight wanted Gabrielle to marry – at some time in the future; she also dearly wanted Gabrielle's help and her friendly presence at Medlicott when it became a hotel. Don't let her go away too soon, she prayed wordlessly.

Howard and Gabrielle rode together, when the weather allowed. Howard said the misty distances of England depressed him somewhat after the brilliance of the Far East. More often, they drove out and occasionally walked, but he declared that he was happy to be lazy with her in their private room at the hotel.

'Why don't you come back with me?' he asked her one

afternoon. 'Stay for two months and return to England with me.'

'Wonderful idea,' said Gabrielle.

'But I mean it. I'm staying with our agent and his wife, and you could stay with them too; and we'd take off now and then for Hong-Kong or Bangkok or Bali. Do come, Gay.'

'But I'm a working girl, Howard.'

'Working girls get holidays, don't they?'

'Not a couple of months.'

'Come for one month, then. You said you couldn't take a holiday in the high season. Well, now it's low season and I'm sure you could get away.'

Gabrielle was also sure she could get away, and the idea was a fascinating one, almost irresistible. So she could not quite explain, even to herself, why she should play for time.

She was having breakfast with Howard in the private room one morning when her father came in.

'By the way, Gay, the Willises have moved out of the old cottage if you're still interested in it. They went yesterday and Mrs. Willis has left everything very presentable.'

It was difficult for Gabrielle to get back to the position where she had been so deeply involved with Mrs. Sanders and her troubles. She had sent flowers twice to the hospital, but after Howard's arrival she had neglected her. Now her conscience reproached her.

'Of course I'm still interested in it, Dad,' she said. 'When can I take over?'

'Whenever you like.'

'I've picked out some stuff to be taken over there from the barn. Do you want to approve before I take it?'

'I suppose I'd better,' said her father.

Gabrielle told Howard why she wanted the cottage and for whom she wanted it; and he offered to help her set it up during the morning. She commandeered the hotel van and had Jim load up the furniture she had chosen and drive to the cottage. She and Howard sat in the back.

'When did you last have such an undignified ride?' she asked him.

'In foreign countries, one has all kinds of undignified rides,' he said.

He did not think much of the cottage and was inclined to agree with her father that it was not fit to live in.

'I don't know,' said Jim. 'Millie and I lived in it for years, it's what you're used to, I suppose. You'd be surprised how cosy it can be with a fire in the range or in the inglenook there. Bit o' carpet on the floor and curtains up at the windows, you wouldn't know the place. And the furniture is better than ever *I* had.'

They did more than put carpet on the floor and curtains at the windows. They carried in tables and chairs, bedsteads, pots and pans, china and glass; all thrown out by the hotel, all much more luxurious than anything the Sanderses had known. Gabrielle had remembered heavy door mats for back and front; fuel for those fireplaces, provisions for the cupboards. The kitchen had a stone sink, a kitchen range, a dresser against one wall; all things that the quarry cottage had lacked.

'Now I must ring up Dr. Huwlett and find out where all the Sanderses are at present,' she said.

She rang him up at lunch time and he answered himself.

'Ivor, this is Gabrielle. How are you?'

'Fine, thanks. And you?'

'Oh yes. I rang up to say the cottage is all ready for Mrs. Sanders and her brood.'

'Good. . . . . I thought you'd forgotten all about us.'

'Not at all. When I say I'll do a thing, I do it. The

Willises only moved out yesterday.'

'Is there furniture there? Beds for them to sleep on?'

'I've been the whole morning setting it up. They can move in this afternoon if they like.'

'Then they certainly will. That place up there is running with damp, and I'll be glad to get *one* little problem off my hands. . . . Gabrielle!'

'Yes?' A little tartly, because he seemed to be taking a great deal for granted.

'I'm enormously grateful to you. I don't know how you did it, or what it cost you, but you moved fast; and I do appreciate it.' Gabrielle was, for once, lost for words. 'And I also appreciate your driving Pat up to the quarry that night. It wasn't easy at all on such a filthy night. If I said anything that seemed sarcastic to you, please forgive it. It wasn't how I felt, I assure you.'

'Oh, that's all right,' said Gabrielle awkwardly, still strangely lost for the right words. 'Will you be there when the family moves in, Ivor?'

'I could be,' he said. 'Will you?'

'I'd like to be. I'd like to see their reaction.'

'Right. Then I'll bring them along myself. They have to be gathered together first. Let me see, there's one urgent call I must make after lunch. Shall we say half past three?'

They arranged to meet at the cottage at that time, and Gabrielle rang off. She told the family what she had arranged, and was surprised to find that Howard intended to accompany her.

'Oh, Howard, you wouldn't be interested,' she said, oddly reluctant for him to be there.

'Everything you do interests me,' he assured her, and she could not think of any reason to deter him.

The doctor was there first, with the Sanders family. Gabrielle arrived a few minutes after him. As she stepped

139

from her car, all the children gathered round her. Ivor, about to follow them, restrained himself as he saw Howard get out of the car too.

There was a babble of talk as Gabrielle made for the cottage door. She opened it with the key, and turned to present the key to Mrs. Sanders with a flourish. The children were about to troop inside when Ivor called them back. 'Wipe your feet,' he commanded. 'You're not going into your new house without wiping your feet, are you?'

They were not to be restrained for long, however; they scampered about, upstairs and down, exclaiming, occasionally shrieking. Mrs. Sanders stood in front of the fire in the kitchen range with tears streaming down her cheeks. The new baby was in her arms, but there was a cot for him too. The kettle was singing on the hob – a piece of Jim's handiwork, for he had been looking out for their arrival.

'You must all 'ave a cup o' tea,' said Mrs. Sanders suddenly. She gave the baby to Gabrielle, who took him gingerly and looked doubtfully at Ivor. Ivor laughed and helped to get the tea. 'Biscuits in the tin,' said Gabrielle, and the children came running for biscuits. They toasted each other in tea, and wished Mrs. Sanders well in this house.

'It's a dream,' she said. 'The kids can go to school. Nobody can turn us out, can they?' Gabrielle shook her head. 'And Dr. 'Uwlett says there's no rent to pay. Well, it's a dream, that's what it is.'

'And mind you keep it presentable for when Sid gets back,' said the doctor.

'I don't reckon 'e'll come back, doctor.'

'Yes, he will. He won't let you down. Well, I've got to be getting along. Bobby, Jessie, Shirley!' The older children looked at him anxiously. 'Mind you help your mother. I'm going to ask her, next time I come, which of you has been behaving properly. Gabrielle, I have to go. You know what I feel about all this. Nelmes,' he nodded at Howard.

'We're coming too, Ivor. Good-bye, Mrs. Sanders. Good luck. I'll come and see you. Good-bye, children.'

They left together. Gabrielle smiled at Ivor – 'With all her charm,' he thought drily.

'So the good fairy waved her wand,' she said, 'and they all lived happy ever after. At least, I hope so.'

He looked at her sombrely. He was angry with himself for being so disappointed that she had brought this man along with her. It was out of this disappointment that he found himself saying: 'This family is lucky, but it's only one. I had hopes that there would be a great many more.'

She looked at him blankly for a moment, and then realized that he was referring to Medlicott House.

'Oh, there's absolutely no pleasing some people,' she cried, whipped up to sudden anger. 'Let's go,' she said to Howard. 'He's spoiled it all. He's impossible.'

She went away to her car, and Ivor to his. Gabrielle left first, Howard sitting beside her. 'I'm sorry,' she said to him. 'He makes me so angry,' and Howard wisely left her in peace.

As Gabrielle drove back to the Tudor Rose, her anger slowly cooled. She still felt that the doctor was impossible; but the thought came into her head that all the things he wanted were for other people – never for himself. He had wanted Medlicott House for other people. She had never really taken into account his disappointment over that. He had not mentioned it, so she had conveniently ignored it. Miss Medlicott had said that he was very quiet when she told him her decision. That he was very quiet for a long time; and that then he had said: 'Well, that's that.'

He had had to accept it, but he had not liked it. A dream he had might have become reality, but it did not. He had taken it quietly, but Gabrielle saw now that he must have been thrown into depths of disappointment.

He probably saw this thing she had done for the Sanders family as a sop to her conscience. Gabrielle was quiet and thoughtful, wondering if what the Knight family thought of as a generous gesture was, in fact, an act of atonement.

CHAPTER SEVEN

HOWARD wanted to carry Gabrielle off to London. There was no doubt that, after the Christmas festivities, when the hotel had been full to capacity and the Knight family had been extremely busy, life in the country at this time of year was too quiet for him.

Her parents persuaded her to go.

'This is the quietest time of year for the hotel. We don't need you, Gay, and we aren't going away ourselves because we want to press on with Medlicott. And Catherine is here.'

So she agreed to go, and looked forward to some gaiety in the theatres, restaurants and night clubs of the capital. Her father gave her a generous cheque. 'You've earned it, Gay, you've been a great help and an added attraction ever since you came home.' So she looked forward too to the buying of new clothes, the whole business of shopping.

When they left, in Howard's fast car, the countryside was almost unbearably beautiful. It had snowed for two days, and the hills were white with the sun glinting on the snow. Bare trees cast graceful shadows on the snow, shadows that were pink and purple. 'If we stayed, we could ski,' said Gabrielle, but Howard said it wasn't any good for skiing and they left. 'It will do her good to have a break,' said her father, but her mother was anxious: anxious that Howard would persuade Gabrielle into marriage, or that he might press for it to be too soon.

They were going to stay with Howard's parents. This had surprised Gabrielle, who knew that Howard had a flat in town. Now it appeared that his flat was at the top of his parents' house, self-contained; and that he did, in fact, spend a good deal of time with his parents, often dining with them.

It surprised her, too, that the house should be so grand. In an exclusive and decidedly expensive district, it was a tall and rather narrow London house, the first floor drawing-room running from front to back, a veritable treasure house; the walls silk-covered, chandeliers of sparkling crystal, every piece of furniture, Gabrielle was sure, a sought-after antique.

Her bedroom followed the same pattern. Luxury was here. Yet it was comfortable and homely, too. Howard's parents were welcoming and gentle, Howard was obviously the apple of their eye, and his friends were received with pleasure. The whole family was cared for by a quiet, pleasant and efficient staff. People grumbled about the difficulty of getting servants in these modern days, Gabrielle reflected, but did they, in fact, get the staff they deserved? The Nelmes family was positively cosseted. If it had not been for the fact that Howard and Gabrielle were so often out, she felt that she would have smothered in so much gentle and expensive comfort.

Going out with Howard was fun. He had tickets for a film première which proved to be a glittering affair with film stars hogging the TV cameras and trying to outdo each other in the matter of clothes and jewels and coiffeures. He had seats for the opera – another gala occasion. His firm had a small permanent block of seats, so that overseas visitors or any important client could be entertained at the opera. He took her to restrained parties, and others that were more fun. They went out to dinner at the places that were the latest craze, and once or twice they had dinner upstairs in Howard's flat with friends of his own age and choosing.

One day, when Howard and his father were at a board

meeting and lunching with fellow directors afterwards, Gabrielle lunched with Mrs. Nelmes, and they went to her private sitting-room for their coffee. Gabrielle supposed that in earlier days it would have been called a boudoir. It was elegant and comfortable, and a set of graceful chairs had tapestry seats of her hostess's making. Gabrielle admired them dutifully.

'I've had a great deal of time, in places all round the world, to wait for my husband when he has been engaged on business. Hence the tapestry,' Mrs. Nelmes told her.

'Have you always travelled with your husband?'

'Usually, yes. He always liked me to be with him.'

'Did Howard go with you?'

'Well, not at first. He had a nanny to care for him here; and then of course he was away at prep school and then public school. But if we were away for any length of time, he flew out to join us for holidays; and later, when we found he was interested in the business, of course he came with us.'

Always with a silver spoon in his mouth, thought Gabrielle, but left to other people to bring him up. Had he ever known hardship? she wondered. Had his mother ever done a hard day's work in her life They lived in luxury here, and probably travelled in luxury too. They were cultivated and pleasant people; and Gabrielle wondered why she did not admire them more.

'I must tell you,' Mrs. Nelmes said with a shy smile, 'that my husband and I have been so delighted to meet you, Gay. It was so obvious all last summer that Howard had met somebody who was absorbing all his attention; and when he insisted upon flying home for Christmas, we knew that it must be quite serious. So we really were quite eager to meet you; and I hope you won't think it an impertinence if I tell you that we both like you very much indeed.'

'Not at all, I'm pleased and flattered,' said Gabrielle.

'Howard tells us that there is a possibility of your flying back with him to Singapore.'

'Oh, I haven't really decided yet,' Gabrielle said hastily. Mrs. Nelmes looked so surprised that Gabrielle realized that it had not occurred to her that Gabrielle might refuse this invitation. 'Of course it would be a wonderful trip,' she added, 'and I've never been to the Far East.' But it would tie me more tightly to this family, Gabrielle thought; and did not feel quite ready to be drawn into the net which seemed to be closing ever more closely and closely around her.

She had never worn so many glamorous clothes in such a short space of time. Evening-dress occasions were occurring constantly, and during the day she must be well turned out. The clothes she had brought with her were not enough; she was glad of her father's gift which made it possible for her to go to fashion shows and boutiques, and buy more. She spent far longer each day than ever in her life before making herself beautiful: scented baths, make-up, visits to the hairdresser, changing into dresses made of expensive materials in glowing colours.

Howard was proud of her. 'You grow lovelier every day,' he told her, meeting her in his mother's drawing-room to have a drink with his parents before going out. His parents, smiling on them both, thought they made a handsome and striking couple.

Gabrielle's breakfast tray was brought to her room each morning. Apparently, early morning was not a social time in this house. The tray was a marvel of elegance and hospitality, and occasionally some letters for her accompanied it. When she saw one addressed to her in her mother's handwriting, she opened it without curiosity; but inside she found another envelope addressed to herself, with an explanatory note from Mrs. Knight.

Dear Gay,

This letter arrived for you several days ago, and instead of putting it in the mailbox at once, I put it in my handbag – with disastrous results! Because I forgot about it. I do hope it is not anything important.

Don't stay away too long – we miss you, and send you our love ...

Gabrielle opened the second letter, turning it over casually to see the signature. Ivor. Ivor! At once she felt a charge of excitement. What could Ivor be writing to her about? With interest, she turned back to the beginning.

My dear Gabrielle,

I never write a letter if I can help it, and rarely write one if a telephone call will do. But it seems to me that, on this occasion, a telephone call will *not* do; because whenever we speak to each other, we seem to get off on the wrong foot, and I make you angry, or you make me angry, and we seem continually to be going back to square one.

So I have taken up my reluctant pen to explain a couple of things, about which I have given a wrong impression or you have been under a misapprehension. God, I'm getting pompous! But I won't start again or I shall get to that state where I fill up the waste paper basket with false beginnings.

First. I admit that I haven't the slightest right to interfere with anything you do, or even to express an opinion, which it seems to me I *have* been doing inexcusably. This ministering angel or fairy godmother thing. You thought it was sarcastic, which it wasn't meant to be, and I apologize: you were offended, and I never wanted to offend you: but do realize that to the Sanders (and even to me) this is rather how you appear: a beautiful being from another world.

Then Medlicott House. Yes, I wanted it, and I was full of chagrin and disappointment at not getting it, although I know it would have involved me in endless schemes for getting money, and endless disputes and consultations with Councils and Ministries. But Joe Buss was an impartial judge and his verdict was probably right. (You see, I have to put in that 'probably': I can't say it outright.) But I shouldn't try to burden *you* with a feeling of guilt about it. You have your life and I have mine, and I, lord pity me, seem to have got involved with the underdog, the underprivileged.

So please accept my apology for all those things I should not have done: and next time we meet let us count ten before we speak to each other – and though this is going to impede spontaneous conversation, it ought at least to be safe.

My mother tells me that you said you would come to supper one evening. Make it soon,

Yours, Ivor.

Sid Sanders is back with his loving family; and adequate explanations and some money. Keep your fingers crossed for them. If I can persuade her to be sterilized, they may have a chance of a life together!

Gabrielle put the letter down and stared thoughtfully into space. This was, without doubt, an offer of friendship. It was handsome of him to apologize. He had made her angry, but only briefly, and now he had apologized. But why did he offer her this friendship, or reconciliation, or whatever it was? Why did he second his mother's invitation to visit them? Simply his sense of fair play? Was he offering the kind of comfortable relationship he seemed to enjoy with

Pat Harper? She could not be sure. She only knew that it had required effort on his part to do this; that he must have been thinking of her, and wanted to stand well with her.

She turned her attention to the breakfast tray, but she poured coffee absently, her thoughts back at Mereworthy Lake, and the Tudor Rose and the lonely hills and the beautiful grounds of Medlicott House, and all the people there.

That day, she and Howard drove into Hertfordshire, to a beautiful country house where his aunt and cousins lived. It was a pleasant occasion, but Gabrielle thought the conversation never came alive. The aunt was Mrs. Nelmes' sister, and had the same air of having been reared in cotton wool and always protected from life in the raw. They were gentle and cultivated and simply null, she thought.

In the evening, back in London, she changed into the most beautiful of her dresses to go to dinner at the house of one of the partners in the Nelmes' business. Another beautiful house expensively furnished. More beautifully dressed people, all apparently charmed to meet Gabrielle. Suddenly she felt like an animal in the ring at a cattle market. She thought that Howard was making sure that everybody approved of her before committing himself, and pride and indignation arose in her.

As if the seal of approval had indeed been put on her by the day's events, Howard stayed behind in the drawing-room with Gabrielle when his parents had gone to bed.

'A nightcap, Gay?'

'No, thank you.'

He came to stand beside her, smiling down at her.

'Darling Gay, I can't put off my flight any later than next week. You are coming back with me, aren't you?'

Hesitation held her back.

'I ought to jump at the chance,' she said at last.

'Then why don't you?' Still with that charming smile.

She looked at him with a doubtful shake of the head.

'Would it make any difference if we went out engaged to be married?' he asked her. 'Will you marry me, Gay? We could be married in the spring when we return . . .' He took her into his arms. 'I do love you, Gay; and everybody who has met you is quite charmed with you. Do say that you'll marry me.'

'Howard, let me think about it a little.'

'Why do you need to think? You must have thought of it already.'

'There wasn't anything definite . . .'

'It was definite enough on my part to bring you back to meet my mother and father – who are already fond of you. But think about it if you want to; and make up your mind to come with me next week. . . . We could have a wonderful time there, Gay, so much to show you, such marvels . . .'

'I know,' she said. 'Can you imagine how I could hesitate?'

'Marriage is quite a step,' he said.

'I was referring to the trip, Howard.'

'Well, I hope you're going to accept both, darling.'

He kissed her and she put her arms round his neck and kissed him back. I have to know what I really feel about him, she thought.

Next morning on her breakfast tray there was a note from Howard, which explained that he had to put in an appearance at his office again, and hoped that Gabrielle might enjoy a day of shopping. Gabrielle, however, had no intention of shopping. When she had breakfasted and dressed, she rang him up.

'Howard? I hope I'm not disturbing anything important?'

'Not at all, Gay. Is there something I can do for you?'

'No, thank you. Howard, I think I shall go home today. Will your mother understand if I make a sudden departure?'

'I'm sure she will, but why do you want to go?'

'For one thing, I want to think about what you proposed last night . . .'

'Can't you do that here, Gay?'

'Yes, but also, *if* I am coming with you next week, there are things I have to arrange, and also I must tell my parents.'

'Of course. Yes, I see, but I don't like that "*if*", Gay.'

'Oh, Howard, I'm not used to dashing off half-way round the world. In my circle, it needs thinking about.'

'*When* you marry me, darling, you'll get used to it.'

Gabrielle packed, rang up the station, rang up her mother to meet her train, by which time Mrs. Nelmes had appeared, and Gabrielle explained her departure – without, however, mentioning the proposal of marriage.

Mrs. Knight was at the station with the car, and they drove towards the Tudor Rose.

'Well, how was it, Gay?'

'Oh, you can't imagine how grand! The power of money! And the Nelmes seem to have plenty of it. Of course, one realized that Howard was comfortably off, and well educated and much travelled, all that sort of thing; but not that he was raised in the lap of luxury. Tickets for film premières, seats at the opera, the best tables in restaurants . . .'

'Well, was your head turned by all this luxury?'

'I hope not. . . . It was fun while it lasted.'

'You speak as if it's come to an end.'

'It's up to me, Mums, whether it's come to an end, or is

just beginning. As far as Howard's concerned, it's just beginning. He wants me to go to Singapore with him, and fly about to Hong Kong and Bali, etcetera. At first he said two months. Now he has agreed to one month – and he's going next week.'

'And you?'

'It seems too good an opportunity to miss. But – '

'But what?'

'There are strings. He wants me to marry him.'

'I knew it!'

Gabrielle laughed.

'It's not the end of the world, darling.'

'No, and we do like Howard; and of course you'll get married, only I hoped it wouldn't be too soon.'

'Well, I've come home to think about it. *I* like Howard, too. And I like travelling. And I suppose I like the idea of being rich.'

'But there are buts?'

'Mmm. I do so love it here, the hills and lake and Tudor Rose and Medlicott; and I was looking forward to all the alterations there. But still, one can't have everything.'

They went on in silence and turned from the town road on to the lake road. The snow had disappeared from the hills and they were clad in their dun winter coat again. The lake was grey today, blown into crisp wavelets by the wind.

'Gay,' Mrs. Knight said at last. 'You said you liked Howard.'

'Yes, I do.'

'I don't want to pry, but shouldn't it be more than that?'

'Yes, I'm sure it should, and I think it might be; and I thought a month of travelling with him, and staying in his agent's house, might sort of clarify the position.'

She tried to clarify the position in her own mind during

the following days. There was little for her to do in the hotel, and she rode over the hills or walked over them trying to decide her future.

She was surprised by her extreme reluctance to leave this place. She had, after all, worked away from it for several years; but now it seemed Home to her; the definitive place to give her comfort and happiness; the place to which, however often she travelled to far-sounding places with strange-sounding names, she would want to return.

One morning she took her car and drove to Medlicott house. Susan informed her that Miss Medlicott was over at the coachhouse, and that if Miss Knight cared to go over, she, Susan, would bring the sherry quite soon.

Gabrielle walked to the coachhouse. Both Susan and Cook were moving over with Miss Medlicott and were looking forward to the change. She found the front door open, and walked inside, closing it behind her. Pieces of furniture were standing in the hall, waiting to be moved; and the sound of voices came from one of the rooms. Gabrielle did not need to be told that Mr. Buss was here again.

'May I come in?' she asked at the open doorway.

Once again there was a hurried rolling-up of large plans. As the coachhouse was completed, Gabrielle could only assume that these were plans of Mr. Buss's new big job.

'Gabrielle, my dear, how pleased I am to see you. I thought you were in London. Do come in.'

Mr. Buss was fitting elastic bands round several tubes of plans.

'Mr. Buss!'

'Yes, Miss Ivy?'

'I think I am going to confide our secret to Gabrielle. I can't keep it to myself any longer.'

Gabrielle looked quickly at her. Surely not! she thought.

What an extraordinary match! It seemed positively incongruous.

'What do you think, Mr. Buss?'

'It's entirely up to you, Miss Ivy. You're the one in charge.'

'Then I shall. Oh, here's Susan with the sherry.'

They waited in silence while Susan came in, left the tray with the sherry and biscuits and Mr. Buss's large tankard of beer. Miss Medlicott waited until she had gone again and then raised her glass.

'To the success of our little enterprise,' she said.

They all drank to it. 'But I would like to know what I'm drinking to,' said Gabrielle.

'Ah, our little secret.' Miss Medlicott smiled benignly on Mr. Buss. 'Well now, Gabrielle, you knew that last summer I was undecided what to do about Medlicott House? I was, in fact, in quite a quandary. My sympathies were really, as I think you knew, with the doctor and his aims; but Mr. Buss was very realistic and pointed out how unsuitable and how expensive they would be, those flats for old people – and you know what decision we ultimately took.

'But something Mr. Buss said gave me an idea. He said it would be far better to start from scratch and build new and convenient places for old people; and it occurred to me, but not for some time, that that was just what I could do.

'I had the money from the sale of Medlicott House. I had considerable amounts from the wills of my sisters. And I thought what a splendid memorial it would be to their dear memory to build for those isolated and lonely people the doctor told me about. Mr. Buss has been my accomplice throughout, and we have the plans complete: we have chosen the site, and there is only one thing to stop us going ahead.'

'And what's that?' asked Gabrielle.

'Planning permission.'

'But surely that's one of the most important things?'

'Yes, but we don't anticipate any difficulty. Mr. Buss has been putting out feelers. You see, Gabrielle, this is my surprise for the doctor. I thought he took our decision about Medlicott most courageously; and he didn't let it affect his attitude to me: in fact, I go to dinner with him and his mother and they come here to dinner with me. Nor did it affect the work he is always doing for unfortunate people. But as he is on many of the Councils or committees, he would have known at once if we had applied for planning permission; and I want to be able to present him with the site and the plans as a great surprise. And I hope he will be one of the Trustees of the place when it is done.'

'What a super idea,' said Gabrielle. 'Where do you plan to have it?'

'Further along the lake, still on my property: on part of the grounds that was not sold to your parents. And now you see why that new vista to the lake was not made; because the hotel people will not be able to see anything of the flats, which will be on one floor, anyway – and vice versa. I remember, my dear, that you yourself said the old people would never get a site like Medlicott. Well, now they have one very like it.'

'And when do you plan to tell Ivor, Miss Medlicott?'

'We thought we would arrange a dinner party – my first in this house – at the end of next week. Dr. Huwlett and his mother, Mr. Buss and myself and you and your parents, Gabrielle. I suppose it is rather melodramatic of me, but I want to present the plans to Dr. Huwlett with a certain ceremony.'

'Oh,' said Gabrielle. 'I don't think I shall be here at the end of next week.'

'You *must* arrange it, Gabrielle. We simply must have you.'

'I'm probably flying to Singapore next week, for a month's visit to the Far East,' and Gabrielle thought how terrible it was to be torn in two directions.

Miss Medlicott looked disappointed, even woebegone.

'I *shall* miss you,' she said.

'We *all* will,' said Mr. Buss, so heavily accenting the word that Gabrielle wondered who was included in it.

'Is it Mr. Nelmes you are going with, Gabrielle?'

Gabrielle admitted that it was, and thought her hostess looked even more disappointed.

'I haven't absolutely decided,' she said.

'Then don't go – or go later, Gabrielle.'

'I suppose I could do that,' said Gabrielle slowly.

It seemed important to her that she should be at this dinner party. 'It couldn't be moved forward a bit?' she asked hopefully.

'I don't see how. I don't move in completely until next week.'

Gabrielle drove home still undecided what to do. It was difficult to decide against the Far Eastern holiday, with its innumerable attractions, yet if she went it would be a stepping stone towards marriage with Howard; and she needed time to think about that. She went into the Tudor Rose, but none of her family seemed to be about. She looked into the bar, and as her father was there talking to Tony, she went to join him.

It was then that she saw Pat Harper, sitting by herself at one side of the huge glowing fire, and immediately made a diversion to go and speak to her.

'Hallo, Miss Harper, are they looking after you?'

Pat indicated the glass at her side.

'I was absolutely perished,' she said, 'so I came in for a drink to warm me up; and this fire is gorgeous. I'm just thawing out.'

'It is cold today.'

'It's not just the day. I've been sitting in an icebox of a little parlour, playing at being a psychiatrist.'

'That sounds interesting. Not the icebox, the other bit.'

'It wasn't interesting at all. Ivor has a young patient who is suicidal. She had a go last summer at cutting her wrists. He thinks she's getting to the point where she'll try it again. She thinks she hates her parents, her work, her workmates and the whole village. Just about everything on God's earth except perhaps Ivor. Well, he's so busy and he's spent hours on her already, so he asked me if I'd see if I could get anything out of her. He thought I might just strike lucky and get a clue as to what's eating her.'

'And did you?'

'Not a hope,' said Pat. 'She clammed up on me. I don't know how Ivor keeps his patience with some of these people. I've got endless patience with my usual cases; but although I know girls like this one are suffering just as much in their way, I feel like giving them a good slap and telling them to wake up. Anyway, it didn't work, and only made me frozen and disgruntled.'

'Let me get you another drink.' Gabrielle came back with the drink and some small, piping hot sausage rolls. 'A filler until your lunch time,' she smiled. 'How is Ivor?'

'He's O.K. Overworking, of course. In the end, he'll have to have a partner, or split up the practice. Haven't you seen him lately?'

'I've been in London for a holiday.'

'Ah, the bright lights. I could just do with some of that myself.' She sounded dejected, as she well might be, thought Gabrielle, after struggling with a suicidal girl in a dreary cold village parlour. It occurred to her that if anybody should be at the dinner party with Ivor it should be Pat.

A day or two later, having been to dinner with two of her

friends recently married, she was driving home along the lakeside road when a car behind gave a prolonged and imperious tooting of its horn. Gabrielle pulled in to the side of the road to let the impatient driver pass, but as he did so, he braked so that Gabrielle had to brake also, and pulled in front of her to stop her, so that she thought it must be a police car and wondered how she had offended. Next moment, however, she realized that it was Ivor's car.

Ivor was walking back towards her.

'Hallo,' he called, as he approached. Then, at the side of the car: 'I haven't seen you for a long time. How are you?'

'Fine,' she said.

'Why didn't you answer my letter?'

'I've been away,' she said. 'In London.'

'I presume you can write in London?'

'My mother didn't forward it for some time, I'm afraid.'

'Excuses, excuses,' he said. 'And you were coming to have dinner with us one evening.'

'The same excuse,' she said. 'I've been away.'

'But you've been back several days. Everybody has been telling me so. Pat Harper, Miss Medlicott, Mr. Buss. Everybody knew except me.'

'Well, now you know too.'

'I've been hearing other things about you as well.'

'Such as?'

'It's cold out here,' he said. 'May I come in?'

'Certainly. I'll just pull in behind your car.'

She did so, and he joined her in the front seat of the car.

'You look very glamorous,' he said. Her fur coat, hanging open, revealed her yellow dress of stiff silk.

'I've been out to dinner. And you, I'm sure, have been working.'

'Alas, I never seem to do anything else. Poor old chap

with a second stroke. You make such a pleasant contrast, Gabrielle, young and beautiful and all dressed up.'

'The tired doctor's antidote.'

'I need that kind of antidote all the time,' he said.

'What are the things you've been hearing about me?'

'Ah.' She had almost forgotten his way of drawing out that 'ah'. 'You are being carried off to the wicked and mysterious East. Somebody is luring you away to haunts of vice and opium dens. Is that right?'

'No, you have it all wrong.'

'You're not going?' he asked, in a more serious voice.

'Well, yes, I'm probably going. I meant you were wrong about the opium dens. It will be quite fascinating, but at the same time highly respectable and extremely luxurious.'

'Good for you,' he said absently. There was silence in the car for some time. At last he said: 'Is it Howard Nelmes, Gabrielle?'

'Yes.'

'Are you engaged to him?'

'No.'

'Are you going to be?'

'I don't know.'

'Has he asked you?'

'I feel as if I'm in a court of law,' Gabrielle said.

'Yes, you're on trial, and I'm cross-questioning. Has he asked you?'

'Mind your own business, Ivor.'

'Now you didn't count ten before you said that.'

She counted rapidly up to ten, aloud, and repeated:

'Mind your own business, Ivor.'

'I'm making it my business. You belong here, Gabrielle.'

'Am I not entitled to a holiday?'

'Undoubtedly. I'm not talking about holidays. I'm talking about you getting engaged to this man, and then married to him, and then leaving us altogether. Are you in love with him, Gabrielle?'

'My goodness,' she cried, 'can't a girl have any private life? Is nothing sacrosanct?'

'Just one little word,' he said, and his voice was quiet. 'Just one word, Gabrielle. Yes or no.'

'It can't be answered in one word, anyway.'

'Why not?' and his voice was suddenly sharper. 'If you're in love, yes. If not, no. Is that so difficult?'

'As a matter of fact, it is,' said Gabrielle. 'There are so many things to take into account.'

'There's only one thing,' he said.

He rested his arm along the back of the seat, and his hand dropped to Gabrielle's shoulder. For a moment, his fingers stroked the fur of her coat, then moved to her cheek and gently turned her face towards him. Gabrielle remained quite still. She knew with one part of her mind that it would be wiser to drive on, yet something else in her wanted to know what was going to happen. His eyes were very dark and his face very serious in the dim light as he drew nearer to her, and next moment she was folded closely in his arms. She did not even struggle. Only when he kissed her did she make a slight withdrawal, which he overcame immediately; and after a few seconds of hesitation, she abandoned resistance altogether, and gave herself up to his firm clasp and his passionate kisses.

She had lost all sense of time when the car's headlights shone on them. They drew slightly apart and turned their heads to see that the approaching car was surmounted by a blue lamp.

'Police car,' said Ivor.

The police car slowed up opposite them, then stopped.

'Gabrielle, we've been copped,' Ivor's voice in her ear was amused, but Gabrielle was not amused. She hated to be found like this.

The police, however, could not have been less interested in her. Through his wound-down window, a policeman's voice said:

'Isn't that Dr. Huwlett's car in front?'

'Yes,' replied Ivor, across Gabrielle. 'Am I wanted?'

'There's been an accident, sir, along the lake.' The man had been present at that earlier accident when Dr. Huwlett had worked on a man under the propped-up car. 'A girl was found in the lake by a young courting couple who parked beside it.'

'Dead?' asked Ivor.

'No, sir, but pretty far gone; one of my mates is giving artificial respiration.'

'Right. I'll get along there.'

'We'll turn and follow you, doctor.'

Ivor kissed Gabrielle swiftly.

'Sorry, darling. My lovely antidote. This could be the impossible Deirdre.'

He was out of the car and into his own, and almost at once off along the road at speed. Gabrielle took a long breath to steady herself, unable to come round from those kisses as rapidly as Ivor, and switched on her engine. The police car flashed past her. She followed to the scene of the accident, but stood by in the darkness.

A small crowd had collected. The police asked them to move on. Already the ambulance had arrived. Gabrielle heard Ivor's voice say: 'I'll have her in the Cottage Hospital, I want to keep an eye on her. Keep it up all the way there,' he said to the ambulance man. Artificial respiration, wondered Gabrielle, or the kiss of life? 'I'll follow you in my car.'

She saw the ambulance move away and the doctor's car follow it. The police mildly advised the small crowd to 'break it up' and left in their own car. Gabrielle drove back to the Tudor Rose but did not go inside at once. She sat in her car, lost in feeling, lost in thought, gazing without seeing at the Tudor Rose on the swinging sign of the hotel.

It was only when a group of young people came out of the saloon bar, arms linked, singing a popular song, that she came out of her brown study. She went into the hotel and straight up to her room, waving to Catherine who was tidying up behind the desk. 'Good night, Aunt Catherine,' she said.

'Good night, Gay. Like some tea sent up?'

'That would be nice,' said Gabrielle without stopping.

She did not want to talk to anybody. She did not want any intrusion into her thoughts just now. Yet, in spite of her determination to get things straight in her own mind, she could not concentrate but drifted continually into the memory of those minutes in the car when, for once, she and Ivor had stopped their verbal sparring; and he, presumably, had decided to find the answer to his own question: was she in love with Howard?

The night porter knocked on her door and brought in her tray of tea. Gabrielle abandoned all efforts to settle her affairs tonight. She would bring a fresher eye and a fresher mind to them in the morning.

'Thank you, Philip,' she said.

'Accident along the lake road tonight, Miss Gay. Girl tried to drown herself. But she chose a bad place for it, where the water was shallow; and a courting couple parked their car at the edge of the lake and saw her in their headlights. It was a second attempt, she tried it last summer by slashing her wrists. Honestly, some of these young kids want shaking up a bit!'

'One never knows what problems people might have,' said Gabrielle, in no mood for gossip. 'Thanks for the tea, Philip.

Good night.'

'Good night, miss.' He went away. He made a practice of talking to everybody, in the hope of instigating a conversation, because the hours of the night were long.

For Gabrielle, who had thought she would lie awake, the night seemed very short. She woke to a clear winter morning of light frost, which soon developed into a day of unusual splendour. After breakfast she went up to her room for a cardigan and stood at the wide window looking out over the sunlit scene. Reflecting the cloudless blue of the sky, the lake was gorgeously blue; and in the stillness of the frosty morning, placid, inviting and calm. The sun was thawing the frost on the bare branches and twigs of the trees, so that they hung with drops which trembled with all the colours of emerald, sapphire, diamond, ruby and topaz before they fell. The hills seemed calm, emerging from a light haze in the distance.

Suddenly Gabrielle knew with certainty and intensity that she did not want to go away. I want to stay here, she thought; and was surprised that she had not known it all along. I would like to stay here for ever.

The admission brought with it a feeling of relief and a glow of content. She pulled the cardigan on over her woollen dress as she looked at the dazzling lake. One would not suspect dark secrets there this morning. She thought of the girl who had been fished out of it last night; a girl who had tried to kill herself last year, probably the girl Pat Harper had attempted to talk to and Dr. Huwlett had spent hours with, and who had tried to drown herself last night.

A sudden idea occurred to her and she hurried downstairs to the telephone at the desk. Two people were reading newspapers by the fire: otherwise the lounge hall was empty, her family busy about its varied affairs. She rang Ivor who would probably be in his surgery at this hour.

He answered the telephone himself.

'Dr. Huwlett,' he said briefly.

'Ivor, this is Gabrielle.'

'And how is Gabrielle this morning?'

'Fine, thank you.'

'I'm sorry about last night, Gabrielle.'

'What are you sorry about?'

'Well, obviously not about what happened between us. Sorry the police came and disturbed us.'

'I hope the antidote did a little good,' she said drily. 'But that wasn't what I rang up about. How is the girl this morning – the one brought out of the lake?'

'She'll be all right in a day or two – physically. Her mental state is something else.'

'I had an idea about that, Ivor. She isn't very successful in her attempts, is she?'

'No. Unlucky, perhaps?'

'Or does she not intend to do it at all? She went into a very shallow part of the lake.'

'And last summer she chose to cut her wrists just before her mother returned home.'

'Could it be – with deference to Your Honour – a way of attracting attention to herself?'

Ivor laughed aloud.

'What's funny about that?' asked Gabrielle, ruffled.

'It isn't funny. I laughed from pure pleasure, because something I suspected has been corroborated. Yes, I agree with you, I think that's what the girl is doing. At least, I thought it last night after this second attempt. But the thing is that we could be wrong, and that she might succeed next time. So, as soon as they have a place for her at Pipfield Park, we'll get her there with a good analyst. Until then, and it shouldn't be more than a few days, I'll keep her at the Cottage Hospital.'

'Well, that's that,' said Gabrielle. 'Are you taking surgery?'

'I am. There are seven or eight patients in my waiting-room.'

'Then I won't delay you, Ivor.' Gabrielle rang off and stood idly at the reception counter. Her mother came into the hall and saw her there.

'Why aren't you out on such a heavenly morning?' she asked. 'We don't need you here. Why not ride?'

'I think I will.' Gabrielle rang up Colonel Reid-Browne, went upstairs to change into riding clothes, and drove to the stables. The Colonel was riding himself, so they went together up into the hills and along the top. The Colonel never wanted to be anywhere but here, with his horses; and since his retirement, refused to go away except for matters of urgency. 'The air really *is* like wine this morning,' said Gabrielle. 'Like champagne.' And she thought of Ivor in his surgery, and of the patients in the waiting-room with their pains and their troubles and their germs. At that moment she felt sorrier for the doctor than for the patients.

'There were two calls for you while you were out,' said her mother. 'One from Mrs. Huwlett and the other from Howard. They're both going to ring again.'

Mrs. Huwlett rang first.

'Ivor tells me that you may be going away next week,' she said. 'So do come to dinner before you go. Sunday is a good day for Ivor – no surgery. Would that suit you?'

Gabrielle said that it would, and that she would look forward to it.

Howard rang up soon after. He wanted to assure himself that Gabrielle's passport was in order and that she had had the recommended inoculations, and came nearer to impatience with her than ever before to hear that these had not been done.

'You're running it fine, Gay. Do get them done at once. And let me know which day you're coming back to town.'

Gabrielle procrastinated. She asked after his parents, she talked of various things, but she neither said which day she would be going to London, nor that she would not be going at all.

Her mother noticed that Gabrielle had done nothing about packing for her trip, although surely by this time she should be making some preparations. Mrs. Knight was torn between what seemed to be a wonderful match for Gay, and wanting to keep her daughter with her, especially when they went to Medlicott House. So she said nothing, leaving Gabrielle to her own decisions; but opening her eyes in some surprise when Gabrielle went off to dinner with the Huwletts on Sunday evening in the yellow dress that was surely too grand for such an occasion.

CHAPTER EIGHT

IVOR admitted her to the house himself. He took her fur coat and ushered her into the living-room which was empty.

'You're the first,' said Ivor. 'My mother is in the kitchen, but she won't be a moment.'

He put his arms round her gently and kissed her.

'You don't have to tell me,' he said. 'I won't spoil your hair, or rumple you.' And kissed her again and then again. 'You owe me this,' he reminded her, 'because we were untimely interrupted the other evening.'

'I don't owe you anything,' she said, but her smile for him was dazzling. 'Is this a good-bye party for *me*?' she asked.

'You're not going!' His grip on her tightened.

'Your mother said that *you* told her I probably was.'

'That was to get you here,' he said. '*Are* you going?'

The doorbell sounded and Mrs. Huwlett called:

'Will you get that, Ivor?'

Ivor let Gabrielle go with a resigned shrug of the shoulders, and went to open the door. He returned with a grey-haired, handsome, middle-aged man who proved to be a surgeon at the big hospital, Robert Keyes. He was followed shortly by a married couple in their thirties, Edwin and Margaret Bond. Gabrielle was pleased to see that Margaret had also dressed up for the occasion. Were there to be other guests? she wondered. No Pat Harper tonight?

The number in the party stayed at six. Ivor proved to be a charming host, dispensing drinks and keeping the conversation lively. 'But no shop,' warned Mrs. Huwlett, and Ivor said: 'Not a word.' Mr. Keyes repeated: 'Not a word.' Edwin and Margaret, it appeared, were going skiing in a few days, which turned the talk to holidays. 'Well, I'm off to Ireland again this year,' said Mrs. Huwlett, 'to my usual cottage. I'm taking it for two months, so anybody who feels like a few days in Connemara is welcome.' Robert Keyes would be sailing in his small yacht. 'Destination as yet unknown,' he said, 'but somewhere where no patients can contact me. What about you, Ivor?'

'No plans yet,' said Ivor, 'but I'd settle for a deserted tropical island.'

'Not quite deserted, surely?' asked Margaret, a small and vivacious brunette.

'I've no objection to a few nut-brown maidens to minister to my wants . . .'

'None of this sounds quite so glamorous as the trip Gabrielle starts on next week,' said Mrs. Huwlett. 'Bangkok, Bali, Hong Kong.'

Gabrielle smiled and caught Ivor's eye. How could she say: I haven't quite decided, with the whole thing only a few days away? She said nothing, listening to the exclamations of the others.

'We really must go and eat,' said Mrs. Huwlett, 'pleasant as this is; because the food will be ruined if we don't.'

They went into the dining-room to a delicious dinner of Mrs. Huwlett's cooking. It transpired that Edwin owned one of the new factories brought into the area. He was a surgical instrument maker. 'So that I'm connected with these two gentlemen,' he said to Gabrielle, 'up to a point; with the advantage that when I leave my office, my work is done.'

'Thank heaven for that,' said his wife. 'I often wonder how doctors' wives survive all these long absences.'

'I think my mother survived pretty well,' smiled Ivor, 'not only my father, but me as well.'

'So would Margaret if she had to. We all adapt to the kind of life we have to live.'

'Constance didn't,' Robert Keyes reminded her; for he and his wife had long been divorced. 'So now I fall in love with yachts instead.'

They talked of sailing; then, by way of the Tudor Rose, came to Medlicott House, and Gabrielle described what was being done. She was so eloquent about its beauties that Ivor said: 'Advertising, Gabrielle; something that, in our profession, we're not allowed to do.'

'Of course I'm advertising. You must all lunch or dine there. It would be a pity to miss the place.'

As they went from subject to subject, all joining in, Gabrielle thought how much more she was enjoying this than some of the dinner parties she had shared with Howard and his parents, or lunches with his relations. Those people had been cosseted and rather dull, jaded about their travels and experiences. Mrs. Huwlett in her enthusiasm for Ireland, Robert Keyes in his for his yacht, seemed much younger than Howard's parents.

They went back to the sitting-room for coffee; and had settled themselves in a circle round the fire when the telephone rang.

'That,' said Robert Keyes, 'will be an accident requiring immediate and lengthy surgery.'

'That,' said Ivor, 'will be an expectant mother.'

'Expecting prompt delivery,' said Mrs. Huwlett. 'I'll answer it, Ivor.'

'No, stay where you are, I'll go.'

He went out into the hall. Mrs. Huwlett continued to pour coffee and her guests to drink it. Then Ivor came back quickly into the room. Robert Keyes looked up at him sharply.

'Cottage Hospital on fire,' said Ivor. 'I'm leaving at once. So very sorry about this, everybody.'

'I'll come with you,' said Robert Keyes, standing up.

'Can I help?' asked Edwin Bond.

'Certainly. We may need able-bodied help. But not you,' to the three women. 'Stay here.'

'How can we, Ivor? There may be something we can do,' said his mother. The men had gone into the hall; and Ivor and Keyes into the surgery and dispensary. The women heard two cars start up on the gravel outside.

'I'd like to go too,' Mrs. Huwlett said to her guests.

'So would I,' said Gabrielle.

Margaret shook her head. 'I'm not much good in this kind of emergency,' she said. 'Accidents, the sight of blood, make me ill – I can't help it.'

'Of course you can't, my dear. Stay here, keep a cheerful fire and keep some coffee hot for us. We'd better take blankets, Gabrielle. The ambulances will have some, but it's bitterly cold for patients taken out into the night.'

They put blankets into Gabrielle's car and set off for the Cottage Hospital which was on the outskirts of the Village on the nearer side. A fire engine rushed past their car, siren wailing. As they drew near, they saw the dense mass of smoke lit by occasional flames and by the light from many cars. One fire engine was already there, its ladder erected. Two ambulances arrived at the same time as Gabrielle. Police were trying to keep a way clear for traffic. 'Keep going, miss,' they said to Gabrielle. 'Make way, please.'

'We're nursing staff,' said Mrs. Huwlett, crisply and inaccurately.

'Pull in here then, miss, behind this one.'

They scrambled out of the car, carrying their piles of blankets.

'Where's Dr. Huwlett?' his mother asked the policeman.

'He's gone in the building with the other doctor.'

They went to the front of the building, where police were

keeping back the crowd. Smoke was pouring from almost every window, and already, so soon after the outbreak of the fire, showers of sparks soared upwards as timber fell in. Another ambulance arrived, the crowd grew thicker, nursing staff off duty arrived to join those that had been on duty, and women from voluntary organizations were setting up the apparatus for making tea.

Two firemen came out of the smoke of the building carrying an old lady carefully between them. Nurses took her from them and wrapped her in blankets, and the ambulance men carried her to an ambulance. A nurse went with her and a woman with tea followed soon after.

Ivor came out carrying a teenage girl. He saw his mother and Gabrielle. 'Here,' he said. 'Wrap her up well, put her in the first ambulance to leave, she's very poorly.'

'You're not going back in there, Ivor?'

'Not when the firemen tell me not to. At the moment there are people not accounted for.'

How could one say, Be careful? wondered Gabrielle. Of course, one couldn't; but she desperately wanted him to take care, not to be under burning beams that fell, or a staircase that crashed. She saw Ivor go back into the building; then she saw a man come out with the help of a crutch, and ran to help him, to put a blanket round his shoulders and lead him carefully across to an ambulance. The first ambulance left for the hospital, patients were being helped into the second; there was a concerted gasp from the crowd as a great burst of sparks flew up into the luridly-lit sky, and a floor fell in. It sounded oddly like the sound made by a crowd at a firework display. Gabrielle supposed that for some people there, looking on, it was an exciting display. Smoke was swept down upon them by the wind in choking clouds, then swept away again. Flames shot up, outlining dark figures of firemen and hospital workers, which vanished again into blackness.

At this moment the crowd was watching the top of the fireman's ladder; for a fireman had rescued a young nurse from the attic floor. She had been terrified already by the fire: now she could not face the descent on the swaying ladder. Carefully the man persuaded her, guiding her feet, holding her; and they came down the last few feet with a rush. The young nurse collapsed in a heap. Her apron was charred, her face was black. Nobody knew if she was injured. She had fainted.

Ivor was at her side, a small space respectfully cleared around him. Skilful hands feeling for damage, studying the smoke-blackened face, feeling the pulse. 'I think she'll do,' he said. 'Take care of her. In the ambulance, to hospital.' The young nurse was carried into the ambulance, another nurse attending her; and Ivor was back at the side of Robert Keyes, examining the caretaker who had fallen when the stairs fell in.

A Sister approached Mrs. Huwlett.

'Ah, Mrs. Huwlett, thank you for your help. I believe we've accounted for everybody. We had twenty-two patients, and they've been counted. And there were only a few of the staff in the hospital. Mr. Keyes and Dr. Huwlett have been wonderful – they were here so quickly.'

'And now the men have to get the fire out.'

'Yes, there won't be much left of the old Cottage Hospital.'

'Such a pity!'

'Well, they won't rebuild it, that's for sure. They've been discussing for a long time if it still had its uses.' Sister's voice was bitter. 'This will settle it.'

'We'll fight,' said Mrs. Huwlett. 'Ivor will, I know.'

'He'll have *my* help, and the help of everybody in the Village.'

Two nurses came up, looking bedraggled and tired.

'What do we have to do tomorrow, Sister?' they asked.

'Well, there's nothing you can do here. You, Nurse Dobson, live in the Village, don't you? You can go home.'

'Nurse Fredericks can come with me.'

'Good, then get off, both of you; and I'll let you know what to do.' The girls set off. Sister said: 'I doubt if we'll have much left in the way of records. Some of the girls come from away, a few of them lived up on the attic floor. They'll have an unpleasant surprise when they come back tonight.'

'I can put up two or three if you need beds.'

'Thank you, I'll remember. Good night, Mrs. Huwlett.'

Sister went away, and seeing doctor and surgeon still engaged on the caretaker, went to help there. Mrs. Huwlett and Gabrielle watched from a distance. Police had kept the crowd well back, but ambulance men, police, nurses, came and went in the chequered light and dark so that Gabrielle caught only occasional glimpses of the two men, concentrated, intense: deliberately oblivious of the crowd. Ivor might say that he had learned to get beyond the dramatic in medicine and surgery, but it was still the aspect that appealed most to the onlooker. The life and death crisis.

At last they signalled to the ambulance. It backed as close to the injured man as possible, and he was transferred with great care to the stretcher and into the vehicle. The crowd was silent as the ambulance went through it and out on to the valley road. They watched the two men stand up and straighten their backs; but now that particular drama was over for them, and they turned their attention to the men who were still fighting the fire.

The police inspector and the fire chief stood with surgeon and doctor. 'Nothing more you can do now, Mr. Keyes, Dr. Huwlett. The worst of it is over.'

'Very old building,' commented the fire chief. 'Went up like tinder.'

'Any idea how it started, Inspector?' asked Robert Keyes.

'None yet, but we'll find out, sir. Great pity; it's done grand service, this little hospital.'

'We'll be off, then, Ivor. Seen Edwin?'

'Around somewhere. Hallo, Edwin, you've managed to get yourself into a mess.'

'You're hardly immaculate. Have we finished here?'

'Yes. We have to round up my mother and Gabrielle.'

Eventually they were all rounded up and returned to Ivor's house. 'I'll go straight on, Ivor,' said Keyes. 'I want to keep an eye on that caretaker. No, there's no need for you to come – there will be others on duty.'

He went on to the hospital. The others went into the house where Margaret anxiously awaited them. She was horrified by their appearance. They had a welcome drink and some hot coffee. 'And I,' said Edwin, 'am going home to have a bath. Come on, Margaret.' And they set off, too.

'And I must go,' sighed Gabrielle.

'In a moment, in a moment.'

They sat wearily by the fire, Ivor, his mother and Gabrielle.

'You've ruined your dress,' said Ivor.

'Yes,' Gabrielle replied. It was completely unimportant.

His face was grimy, his eyes red-rimmed from the smoke. He blinked continually as if they were sore. She ought to go, and let him bath and rest, but there was an atmosphere between the three of them so relaxed and so congenial and understanding that she was reluctant to break it.

The ringing of the doorbell broke it.

'What now?' asked Mrs. Huwlett as Ivor went to answer

it. But she smiled as she saw that two young nurses had arrived, dropped outside by a fire engine which waited until the men saw the girls being welcomed into the house. They were tired and frozen; and were settled into chairs by the fire and given hot coffee. 'We'll make up beds for you presently,' said Mrs. Huwlett.

'May I help?' asked Gabrielle.

'No, my dear, the girls and I will manage.'

'Then I'll get home.' Gabrielle rose to her feet and Ivor rose to go with her. 'I'll drive you home, Gabrielle.'

'Of course not,' she said. 'I have my car here and you must be tired out.'

He went out with her to her car.

'Lovely night,' she said, thinking she could detect smoke in the air. 'But what a night! I'm glad there were no deaths.'

'Until now,' he said.

'Ivor! Were there serious injuries, then?'

'No, no, I shouldn't have said that to worry you. Only the caretaker at least, burns and fractures. Robert will do his best for him.'

'And the little girl, the one you said was poorly.'

'Poor girl, I'm afraid her days are numbered: she has leukaemia.'

'Oh no! How can you sound detached about it, Ivor?'

'My dear, I'm not detached. Not unfeeling, at least. But I have to be practical. The laboratory fellows, the men in research, are the ones to come up with something to combat it. There are people living happily today with conditions that would have killed them less than a generation ago. No, I'm not detached. I treat hopeless cases as well as I can, make them as comfortable as possible. But there are hundreds more I *can* do something for – I get on with that.'

'I spoke without thinking. I didn't count ten.'

'And don't hold *that* against me, darling. I don't want you to lose your spontaneity.'

She opened the car door.

'Good night, Ivor. Go and rest, you must be all in. I hope you don't hear from any expectant mothers.'

'Is that all I get for good night?' he asked.

She took her hand from the door handle, and turned to him with a slight hesitation. Then suddenly she threw her arms round his neck and kissed him on the lips, and he caught her into a violent bear hug, sweeping her off her feet. In a sudden surge of delight and passion, they kissed and kissed again, clinging to each other; but at last he let her go. 'Home to bed,' he said.

'You smell of smoke and disinfectant,' she told him, still refusing to unclasp her hands behind his neck.

'A delightful combination. Let go, hussy, and go home to bed.'

'No,' she said, kissing his cheek.

'All right then,' he said. 'Whose bed shall we sleep in? Yours, or mine?'

That divided them with more speed than his protests. He laughed as she turned towards her car, closed her in, and stood back to watch her turn on the gravel sweep. She waved a hand to him through the window before she wound it up, and soon was nothing but a red rear light vanishing into the distance, until that had disappeared too.

When Gabrielle got back to the Tudor Rose, her parents and Catherine were in bed. There was nobody about but Philip, the night porter, who wanted to keep her talking about the hospital fire. 'Much too tired to talk, Philip,' she said; but she accepted his offer of a tray of tea, because the smoke had made her so thirsty. And when he had brought it to her room and gone again, she had a hot bath, put on a warm dressing gown and sat down at her writing desk, the tea beside her, to write a letter. She might be tired, but she was also stimulated, and this was something that had to be done now, immediately, while she was quite certain in her own mind.

Moreover, Mary (who was to be Catherine's receptionist at the Rose), was going to London in the morning with her mother to spend a week of holiday in a hotel, shopping and seeing the sights. Mary could take this letter with her if Gabrielle did it now; and the sooner it was delivered by hand, the less disturbed she would feel about it.

It was a bulky letter when it was done. She addressed the envelope, added a brief note to Mary, and took it downstairs straight away to Philip, who would see that Mary had it before she left for her train. Gabrielle could not trust herself to be awake early in the morning after the upheaval of this night.

Nor was she. Her mother looked in on her twice during the morning and she was sound asleep. When at last she woke, her mother took in a tray for her, settled herself in an armchair near the bedside for a talk, and said: 'Howard has rung you twice this morning.'

'Oh dear,' said Gabrielle. 'If he rings again, will you tell him I'm not available?'

'Why are you not available? Are you going out?'

'No, but I don't want to talk to him.'

Mrs. Knight raised her eyebrows, but before she could ask a question, Gabrielle said: 'I've written to him. Mary is delivering the letter by hand. I don't want to talk about it, Mums.'

'All right. It seems you had an adventurous evening with the Huwletts, Gay.' And the talk was diverted into safer channels.

Gabrielle was disappointed that she did not see Ivor that day. She had half expected him to rush to the hotel to see her: at least, to ring her up. But neither of these things happened. Her first explanation to herself was that he must be busier than usual, and that he now had another problem to cope with – the rebuilding or replacing of the Cottage Hospital, which everybody seemed to take for granted would not happen.

The second explanation was that, after all, nothing very specific had taken place between them. They had exchanged kisses on a few occasions: last night with more enthusiasm than before. But everybody did that these days, and to attach too much significance to it was being childish. He probably had done that much with Pat Harper – if not more. And with other people. He was in his thirties and it would be surprising if he had not. Yet she could not rid herself of the feeling that something important had taken place. 'Stupid,' she chided herself. 'Important to you, perhaps, but it didn't have to be important to him.'

It was, as it happened, a particularly busy week for Ivor. He had committee meetings to attend, which took up too much of his valuable time, he had two Clinics that week, an increased number of 'flu cases, and a confession from Deirdre which he was doubtful about taking seriously.

It was the Inspector who came to him about that. Deirdre had wept all through the night of the fire and most of the following day. She had then confessed to a nurse that she started the fire at the hospital; and the nurse had reported it to her Sister, who took it further, even though nobody at that stage believed her confession. The kindly Inspector, who already knew her history, treated it as a case of nerves, soothed her, told her not to worry; and went on looking for the real cause of the fire.

Deirdre had been taken to the big hospital with all the other patients from the Cottage Hospital, although Ivor had reserved the first available bed for her at Pipfield Park where she would have been in the hands of psychiatrists and analysts. Now, because Ivor was her doctor, he was expected to take her in hand; and after two long and frustrating sessions with her, he believed that she had indeed started the fire on Sunday evening. With this conviction in mind, he got in touch with Pipfield Park, to which she was transferred at once. 'If they'd taken her in when I asked them to,' Ivor grumbled to the Inspector, 'none of this need have happened.'

'You never know,' replied the Inspector. 'We might have lost Pipfield instead.'

With all this, and more, on his mind Ivor did not particularly want to go to dinner at Miss Medlicott's new house.

'It will do you good, Ivor. All work and no play, you know.'

'What is it – a housewarming?'

'No, she's having a larger drinks party for that, later. It's just a cosy dinner party – you'll enjoy it.'

'Who's going?'

'*You* (I hope) and I. Gabrielle and her parents. Joe Buss.'

'That's a strange mixture. Is Joe doing the work on the hotel for the Knights?'

'No, they have another builder.'

'That makes it stranger still,' said Ivor, but he made no more protests; and on the evening itself presented himself for his mother's inspection, wearing his newest suit, and a pale green shirt with a darker green tie. 'Very nice,' his mother commented.

'Well, *you're* absolutely resplendent,' he told her.

'Gabrielle hinted to me that it was a very special occasion.'

'Whatever's happened? Has old Joe proposed to Miss Ivy?'

He laughed at the idea.

'What's funny about that? Stranger things have happened.'

'Not much. An elephant and a mouse.'

'I don't suppose for a moment it's anything like that. But really, Ivor, sometimes you are so insensitive.'

'It's my profession, darling, that makes me so hard.'

She relaxed and smiled at him and went to kiss him on the cheek, thinking that hard was the last word she would apply to him.

At the newly restored coachhouse, everything and everybody were resplendent. The house was a gem, the atmosphere light, airy, graceful, furnished with all the best things from Medlicott House, but nothing too heavy. It was perfection, the guests agreed, carrying their drinks with them on their short, conducted tour. Mr. Buss was sincerely congratulated. Strange, thought Gabrielle, that such a great bear of a man should have such a sure and delicate touch.

The women had tried to set off the loveliness of the house. Mrs. Knight, pretty, vivacious, always well dressed, could not help but envy the elegance of Ivor's mother and her cool, precise beauty which was at variance with the warmth of her nature. Even Miss Medlicott had a new dress for this occasion, but it was Gabrielle with her youth and her beautiful colouring who stood out.

Over dinner, the combined topics of the coachhouse and the future hotel finally done with, they spoke of the fire at the Cottage Hospital and Ivor told them of Deirdre's confession.

'The newspapers will have it soon,' he said. 'It appears that there will have to be a prosecution.'

'Whatever will happen to her?' exclaimed Gabrielle.

'Oh, it will be a plain case of diminished responsibility,'

said Ivor. 'They'll keep her in the psychiatric unit until this all dies down, or she improves.'

They discussed the girl's motives: (drawing attention to herself, revenge on society); but since only Ivor knew much about this subject and he was disinclined to discuss it, that flagged and died.

'The disastrous fact is,' he said, 'that we are now without a Cottage Hospital, and I don't see a cat in hell's chance of getting it rebuilt.'

'But why not?' asked Miss Medlicott.

'It seems to be the policy of the moment to do without these Cottage Hospitals, and send everybody off to great new shining ones, to which they might have to travel fifteen miles or more. The trouble is that most of the people I get into the Cottage Hospital will never get a bed in the big one. They'll languish in their homes without nursing, or the old ones will get shoved into a geriatric ward.' There was a silence. He looked round the table. 'I'm sorry,' he said. 'My God, I'm sorry. Talk about the death's head at the feast! If I go on like this, I'll be getting bitter and taking to drink like old Pasture. Gabrielle, say something to cheer us all up.'

'I think Miss Medlicott is more likely to do that,' Gabrielle said.

'Yes, I think this is the moment, don't you?' Miss Medlicott asked the assembled company; and when they all agreed, she said:

'We were going to wait until after dinner, Ivor; but if you want cheering up, we'll do it now. Mr. Knight, will you open the champagne? And Mr. Buss, do you have the plans?'

Ivor looked mystified as the two older men went into action. Mr. Knight brought the champagne glasses from the side table and filled them. Mr. Buss went out of the room and returned carrying a long red cardboard tube which he handed to Miss Medlicott. She rose to her feet and made a brief speech shyly and quickly which seemed to be about all Ivor's remarkable qualities; and presented him with the tube.

'Thank you for your splendid tribute,' said Ivor, smiling, 'which was much too good to be true. And what am I supposed to do with this?'

'Open it, of course,' said Gabrielle, and all the others chorused: 'Open it!'

It was opened and the contents unrolled. There was no room on the table to spread out the plans, and Ivor knelt on the carpet and unrolled them there. The others gathered round. Gabrielle put a toe on one corner to hold the plan down, and Ivor read the wording across the top of it. He looked up at Miss Medlicott without saying a word, and returned to the plan to study it at some length. He let the top plan roll itself up again and looked at the one underneath, which was a site plan, showing the flats positioned by the lake. The third was a complicated affair of pipes and drainage and main services: the fourth showed enlargements of plans for individual flats, varying in size and in quality of equipment.

At last Ivor rose to his feet. He went to Miss Medlicott, put an arm about her and kissed her. He shook hands with Joe Buss.

'This must have been going on for a long time,' he said.

'Almost since the day we told the Knights they could buy the house for a hotel,' Miss Medlicott said.

They adjourned to the drawing-room, and Ivor once more spread plans all over the floor, holding them down at the corners with books and objets d'art. Now everybody talked at once: of the Trust, the Trustees, the need for planning permission ('already in hand,' said Joe Buss), the fact that he was ready to start building the moment he had the O.K.

'It's not a nursing home,' said Miss Medlicott, 'nor an old

people's home. It's what you wanted, Ivor, private dwellings where people have a chance to meet one another.'

Ivor's smile seemed to be fixed on his face. His mother said:

'This has put new heart into Ivor.'

'By heaven, it has,' he said. 'If we can do this, we can do more as well.' He was newly charged with energy. 'We can fight for our Cottage Hospital. The Villagers will be solidly behind it. Will *you* all help us too?'

They all agreed to help, but he was looking at Gabrielle and Gabrielle was looking back at him. Her eyes were shining. She was happy because this had made him happy. With difficulty they looked away from each other at last, but for the rest of the evening, they were both waiting for it to end. They drank coffee and liqueurs, they joined in the conversation, but both of them were waiting for the moment when this party would break up.

When it did, and the guests were going to their cars, and Miss Medlicott was waving good-bye from the open doorway of her new house, Ivor said to his mother:

'Will you drive yourself home, Mother? I want to talk to Gabrielle.'

'Of course,' she said, adding to herself only: 'Good luck, my dearest Ivor, good luck.'

She drove off first, into a night lit palely by half a moon. Mr. Buss followed, and then the Knights. Ivor got into the front of Gabrielle's car and, with a last wave to Miss Medlicott, they drove to where the new drive met the drive to the big house.

'Let's go to Medlicott and walk on the terrace,' Ivor suggested.

Gabrielle turned immediately towards the big house. She stopped the car in front of it, and they walked round the side of the house and up by the narrow side steps on to the wide stretch of the terrace. A narrow band of golden light rippled on the surface of the lake, reflecting the moon. An owl called a few times, and then the silence of the night was completely undisturbed.

Ivor put his arm round Gabrielle's shoulder and they began to walk slowly along the terrace.

'So you didn't go to the haunts of vice and the opium dens,' commented Ivor.

'Obviously.'

'Why didn't you, Gabrielle?'

'Because I wanted to stay here.'

'And how did Howard Nelmes take that?'

'I have to admit that I took the cowardly way out and wrote him a letter. But I had a reply this morning; and he took it as one would expect him to, like a gentleman, all regret and courtesy.'

'That sounds rather lukewarm to me. I don't think I would be a gentleman in such circumstances.'

'You and Howard are very different people. To tell the truth, Ivor, I feel very relieved, I found their way of living very stultifying.'

'What, with all that money and all that travelling?'

'Yes. The people were still dull.'

'Why did you want to stay here?'

'Because I really love it here; this place is my home.'

'You turned down Howard for that? You couldn't have loved him much if you love a place better. Haven't you heard "Whither thou goest, I will go" and so on?'

'Yes, well, I didn't love him much. Not at all, in fact. I liked him.'

'When did you discover that? In London?'

'I don't know when. I just know that I don't.'

'Tell me then. When did you discover that you love me?'

'I don't know that either.' She was tired of his teasing and his questioning. She stopped to face him, her voice quiet and serious. 'I only know that I do love you, and I think it must have started way back last summer and it's been growing all the time. I love you so much: and I thought you might be tied in some way to Pat Harper, but just lately I began to feel you must love me.'

'Pat? My darling girl, I've known Pat for donkeys' years. If anything was going to happen between us two, it would have happened before now. Do you know, Gabrielle, I've wanted for years to get married: for one thing, I thought it was time my mother had a life of her own, but she wouldn't leave me while she thought I needed her, although I assured her I'd manage perfectly well with a housekeeper. I've often thought that Robert Keyes has a soft spot for her, in spite of his talk of falling in love with yachts!

'At one time, I admit, I thought it might be Pat. We're very fond of each other, but I suffered from that luke-warmness that I sense between you and Howard, and it just wasn't enough for me. I never found someone I wanted to tie myself to for life. Because, with me, it would be for life: complete domestic bliss with children and all. It's hardly fair to ask you to take it on, Gabrielle. You see how I can't stop working.'

'That's all right,' she said. 'I like you to work.'

'Well, of course,' he said blandly, 'what was *quite* obvious was your growing interest in my work – and in me.' (Gabrielle gasped at his presumption.) 'The Sanderses up in the quarry, old Mrs. Barnes, your ideas about Deirdre . . .'

'If I feel too badly neglected, I can always put my children in the car and go home to Mother and the luxury of Medlicott House, until you come to your senses. She will always have room for us at Medlicott.'

'You mean you're accepting me?'

'You haven't asked me yet.'

'I ask you now.'

'You haven't said yet that you love me.'

'Well, I do,' he said seriously. 'I love you, love you, love you. I can't imagine that I'll ever stop, ever come to the end of it. I only wish I had more to offer you than the kind of life I lead.'

'Whither thou goest, I will go. Thy people shall be my people,' quoted Gabrielle.

'What, all of them? The halt and the maimed, the old and the lonely, the kooky kids who set fire to places, the children who scald themselves and cut themselves with carving knives and fall out of trees . . .?'

'You make it sound like a horror film, darling.'

'Well, I don't ask it of you. I want you to stay young and beautiful and the most glamorous thing in this countryside. I'll reorganize. I'll get a partner and a secretary – maybe. I'll stop trying to be all things to all men – if I can. I want to have time to spend at home with my lovely wife and all my lovely children, even to go away with them sometimes.'

'And just where, I wonder, is "home" going to be?' said Gabrielle, who suddenly wondered if she would be living in Ivor's house with Ivor's mother.

'Ah.' An even longer-drawn-out 'Ah' than usual. 'Now thereby hangs a tale . . . I have an out-of-this-world plot of ground up in the hills, with planning permission laid on. It's been my dream to build a house there, as modern as the minute with all the available sunshine flooding in; and now we'll do it, Gabrielle. It wasn't exactly a gift, although at the price I paid for it, it almost was; and nowadays you just wouldn't get permission to build there. A man bought it many years ago for his retirement, but his wife fell ill and was my patient for two or three years before she died. So the joy had gone out of it for this man, and he seemed to think I had exceeded the line of duty, as they say, in caring for his wife – so there you are.' They stopped their pacing, interlinked, along the wide terrace, and he turned and took her into his arms. 'We'll go tomorrow and look at it, Gabrielle. No, damn it, I can't tomorrow, I won't have the time . . .'

'Never mind,' she said. 'The day after, or the day after that . . .'

They kissed, and could not have enough of kissing. Gabrielle wondered fleetingly how she could ever have considered marrying Howard even for a moment, a man so pleasant and punctilious, so correct and yet so lacklustre. Ivor was none of these things: he would be angry and fight for what he wanted, or enthusiastic and slave for it. He would be delighted and share his delight; and often cast down, and swear about his failures or grieve about his losses. She kissed him with passionate care for him, and saw vaguely, through her present rapture, what dedication meant.

At last they drew a little apart.

'I must take you home,' Ivor said.

'Why? This night is going to happen only once in our lives.'

'Why? Because I'm freezing to death, even if you're bundled up in furs. Come along, darling.'

In the car, she nestled close to him.

'Will Joe Buss build our house, Ivor?'

'Of course. Who else? He's going to have a busy summer, that man, but he'll be equal to it.'

'And I'm going to be busy, what with Medlicott and *our* house. You won't be the only one, Ivor, absorbed in his work. What a gorgeous summer it's going to be!'

He left her in the lounge hall of the Tudor Rose, with Philip in an armchair behind the desk as interested spectator of their loving farewell.

'I'll ring you tomorrow, Gabrielle darling, and we'll go up to our site the day after tomorrow.'

'Tomorrow and tomorrow and tomorrow,' she said. 'All our tomorrows together, Ivor.'

'Starting today,' he said, seeing that the hands of the clock had already unaccountably crept on to half past two in the morning.